CLAIMING HIS FIRE

FERAL BREED MOTORCYCLE CLUB
BOOK FIVE

ELLIS LEIGH

Kinship Press

Claiming His Fire
Copyright ©2015 by Ellis Leigh
All rights reserved
ISBN: 978-0-9961465-2-4

Kinship Press
P.O. Box 221
kinship press   Prospect heights, IL 60070

The author acknowledges the copyrighted or trademarked status and trademark owners of the following wordmarks mentioned in this work of fiction: Zippo.

For the stubborn women of the world,
May you forever keep your eye on what you want,
and may you always get exactly what you need.

ONE

THE NUMBERS ON THE page ran together into illegible black lines. Dates, times, and identifiers no longer recognizable through the heavy anchor of exhaustion pulling me deep. I'd been staring at the same pages for hours, been trying to deduct reason and order in the details they represented for days, but I'd accomplished nothing. Nothing that made sense, that clued me in to where or how or why. I had reached a point where the numbers on the paper only made my head hurt.

"Yo, Shadow. Where ya been?"

Cringing at the thought of all the work left to do, I grabbed a flyer and slid it over my documents before spinning at the familiar voice. A true smile spread unbidden as one of my favorite Feral Breed denmates—one I didn't mind taking a break from work to catch up with—strode toward me.

"Hey, Gates. How's it going?"

The big shifter gave me a traditional welcome—grabbing both my forearms and nodding—before pulling me into a sideways hug. Three solid backslaps later, he pulled away and looked me over, smile falling.

I readied myself for an inquisition. I knew what he saw—I'd

lost a lot of weight and a bit of color over the past few months. My work, the missions I was being assigned to outside of my Feral Breed responsibilities, had taken their toll on me. Hell, they'd taken their toll on all of us involved in the investigation of the numbers on those pages.

Still, I kept my head up and my game face on. If Gates sensed weakness, he'd be all over my ass, which was the last thing I had time for. I needed him to believe that I was fine. Tired and a little stressed, but fine. Strong. Ready. When in reality, I was just too damn stubborn to quit.

"Seriously, man, where have you been?" he asked, still looking concerned. "I haven't seen you since you split off on the road back from North Dakota in February."

I glanced at the paperwork on the bar, the information I'd been reading when he arrived. Columns of numbers in varying lengths, seemingly random. But there was nothing random about the information on those sheets. Each number related to a case, each case to a female shifter who had gone missing, each one important to someone somewhere and possibly in a lot of danger. I couldn't talk about them, though. Not to anyone in my den, at least.

But the secrecy wasn't what made my gut knot and my palms sweat. It was one particular number, one line item, which related to a shewolf named Kaija. A shewolf mated to the man in front of me. Though her kidnappers had failed—thanks in no small part to Gates himself—there was no guarantee they wouldn't come back for her. Something I was sure Gates worried about, and something I couldn't let him know worried the team investigating the kidnappings as well. I just hoped he didn't ask me about the jobs I'd been running because I'd have to lie. And there was no way I could look him in the eye while I lied. Any other man, sure…but not Gates.

I shrugged, intentionally casual. "Nothing man, just working on a couple of things out in Chicago."

The weight of Gates' stare brought my eyes up to meet his. I kept my face solid, giving nothing away as he watched me. The other guys might joke about Rebel's intense stare, how he seemed able to see right inside of them, but Rebel had nothing on Gates. When you caught the interest of the Gatekeeper, you knew it. Hell, I could feel his look all the way down to my toes.

Gates knew the basics of why I'd been spending so much time in Chicago. Blaze—or President Blasius Zenne, leader of the National Association of the Lycan Brotherhood—needed me to help search out information on the missing Omega females that had been popping up. All the guys in my Feral Breed denhouse knew that much. But the rest…well, that was a different story.

The missions I was a part of remained a secret for now, the search methods and data gathering we were using going against a whole hell of a lot of laws, both human and shifter. My objectives were cloaked in secrets, bathed in misdirection, and coated in falsehoods. All things I had experience in. I'd been hiding the truths about myself practically since birth, keeping my heritage a secret so as not to be seen as different or less. What made me *me* could never be public knowledge. Hell, not even Gates could know those truths.

Finally, with a single nod, Gates surrendered to my silence. "So, when did you get back?"

"Last night." I yawned, covering my mouth with the back of my hand. "Sorry. I barely slept. I haven't even had time to unpack my bag yet. Rebel was all up my ass at like seven this morning. Doesn't the man ever sleep in?"

"Charlotte must not be in town." Gates grinned as I huffed a laugh. Everyone knew our club president could be a grouchy old fuck when his mate wasn't around. The couple decided to move her and her teenaged brother Julian to Detroit to live with him, but she'd asked Rebel to be patient until Julian finished the year out at his school. I'm sure Rebel accepted that reasoning, but acceptance didn't mean liking. He wanted her in Detroit...period. Which made him a total pain in the ass to be around when she wasn't.

Gates pulled out a barstool and sat down. "Been riding much yet?"

I pulled up a stool for myself, my shoulders relaxing as he changed the subject. Not that I wanted to lie to my Feral Breed brothers, but when the president of the NALB tells you to keep your mouth shut, you keep your mouth shut. Something I was pretty good at anyway, so it wasn't as if the rest of the guys would notice. But Gates...he noticed much more than most. Especially about me.

"Yeah. I was tooling around Chicago as soon as the snowpack melted." I leaned back and shrugged one shoulder, playing supercasual even as I wanted to dance around like a kid on Christmas morning. "Plus I got my new skid from Yard Shark Customs back in March."

Gates smirked. He knew how much I'd been waiting to get my hands on that bike. It had been the subject of just about every one of our discussions over the last year as his brother tweaked and rebuilt a classic World War II-era ride for me. My wait had seemed endless, but bringing an old Harley-Davidson XA into the twenty-first century without destroying the feel of the ride I remembered from my soldier days had taken precision. Beast was the best, and my new bike was a testament to that fact.

"You been tearing it up out there?"

"A little." I grinned and pointed to the paper at the top of the pile. "And I can't wait to take it out for this. Detroit to Chicago with both dens of the Feral Breed Great Lakes to celebrate Blaze's birthday? Hell yeah, that's my kind of ride."

"Kaija's looking forward to it as well." Gates got the look on his face that he always did when he spoke of his mate. A look that screamed of happiness and love, of lust and desire, with just an edge of I'll-kick-your-ass-if-you-even-think-of-fucking-with-her. Badass in love…that was Gates.

"How's the munchkin doing?" I asked, truly concerned. Kaija, or Princess as we called her, was the first female Feral Breed Motorcycle Club member and topped out at maybe five feet tall on a good day. Tiny but mighty, that was our Princess. She'd only been riding with us for a few months. I'd seen her and Gates on a mission in North Dakota when we had to run a snatch and grab on a human mated to Gates' brother. I'd been too busy with the Omega fiasco to stick around much longer than it took to follow the team back to Chicago, only stopping off to deliver a baby along the way. The others continued driving to Detroit, and I turned off for Merriweather Fields to get back to work.

"Don't let her hear you call her that" —Gates shook his head and grinned— "but the munchkin's doing well. She's taken to this life better than I could have imagined. Though, if she doesn't stop volunteering for every fucking job Rebel needs done, I'm going to have a heart attack."

"Still a little overprotective, bro?"

His eyes turned lighter, nearly glowing, and a soft but menacing growl rumbled out of him. "She's my heart. Wouldn't you be?"

I nodded, agreeing just to make the conversation end. I had no idea what it was like to have a mate. I'd yet to find that other half to my soul, and maybe I wouldn't. My mother's ancestral breed had no such legends of magic and fate tying two people together. They were more the choose-your-own-adventure type than fate-chooses-for-you kind of shifters. They chose their mates, claimed them with their bite, and bonded to them in a more human fashion…if they even chose to stick around. Many didn't, like my mother, who never exchanged claiming bites with my father and left him not long after I was born. Different breed, different standards, apparently. Not that I ever talked about my family history. It was a bit too…unusual, even for a group of men who shifted into wolves at will.

Gates glanced at my paperwork again, frowning, and then purposely let his eyes wander over my face. I sat straight and still, waiting him out. He could probably see the shadows of bruises I'd been sporting, but hopefully he wouldn't ask about them. There was nothing I could tell him about the past few weeks. Not a single, solitary word.

Gates took a deep breath and seemed to tuck away whatever he wanted to say. But his jaw remained stiff, and his eyes still held that hard edge to them, putting me on the defense.

"Think you're going to need to head back to Chicago any time soon?" he asked, not meeting my eyes, his words way too clipped to be casual. "Outside of the ride, of course."

I stiffened instinctually, wary of how far he intended to dig. "That depends."

Gates waited, his long stare feeling much more like a challenge than I wanted to admit. He'd been my friend for years, been my biggest supporter when I began hanging around the den. This sudden friction between us didn't feel right, but it wasn't something I knew how to avoid.

Eventually, when I refused to back down, he sighed and ran a hand through his hair. Frazzled. Very un-Gates-like.

"Look, Shadow. I know you've been given orders by Blaze not to talk about what you're doing out there, but—"

"You're right," I interrupted, my voice flat and my words crisp. "I have. Which means I can't talk about it." I held his gaze, fighting to keep my face as expressionless as I could, refusing to show him even a hint of emotion. Of weakness.

Gates growled again, low and deep. "This shit affects my mate."

"Not right now, it doesn't."

Gates turned away, shifting his glare to some point across the room. "You don't get it."

"Try me."

He spun back, looking somehow less angry and more... scared, almost. A definitive difference from his normal, confident attitude.

"I swore to her that I wouldn't fail, that I'd keep her safe, that they wouldn't..."

He closed his eyes for a second and took a deep breath, his hands curling into fists. "They took her from me. Those bastards had their hands on her. If I hadn't been there, the Fates only know where she would be right now. We didn't have any idea there were shifters kidnapping Omegas before those fuckers made a play for Kaija. You were there with us...fighting by my side to protect her. You knowing shit and not telling me is..."

He paused, shook his head, and looked away. My stomach knotted as my friend, someone I respected and knew as a brave and strong fighter, broke before my eyes. Damn it, this was why I hadn't wanted to come back. Not yet...not until the whole Omega business was solved. With Gates' mate being one of the shewolves targeted, I knew there'd be pressure to speak about things Blaze had deemed top secret. Gates had to be desperate for information. And yes, there was a little buzz about the white wolf Omega who had slipped through the kidnappers' fingers, but there wasn't a whole lot I could tell him. Not without defying orders and betraying the trust of my team.

Still, some men just needed a little reassurance to set their soul at ease.

Giving in to my desire to take care of my brother, I leaned forward and lowered my voice. "Nothing I'm working on affects her directly at the moment. If I found out information like that, you'd be one of the first to hear it, my brother. I'd never let any danger come at her if I could help you avoid it."

Gates sighed, his shoulders sagging. "I know...it's just been such a fucking mess. We can't ever truly be comfortable. Either the guys are giving her a tough time and I have to rein in my need to knock their fucking teeth out, or someone brings up the Omega kidnappings. We've never gotten the chance to just *be*. There's always something hanging over us."

I sat back, silent, the words to reply not within me. Nothing I could say would calm that fear, none of the things I'd learned in medical school could stop his pain. It was something he needed to push through. Something I couldn't help with.

After a moment, he shook his head, looking a little uncomfortable at his admissions. "I shouldn't have pushed you like that. I just hate not knowing what all of you are doing about this. I need details."

"You don't want to know." I kept my face stiff, my eyes locked on his. "You really don't want to know what we're doing, Gates. Just trust me, we're working on it. Every day and night, we're working on tracking these fuckers down."

I dragged the flyer off the top of my stack of papers and pulled one document to the side, taking a glance at the number that represented Kaija. Her stats rolled out in the row following her unique indicator: her birthdate, her pack status, the date of her brush with the kidnappers. But one column in particular caught my attention. The one with a simple three in it. One of only a handful of threes in that column. The indicator of an Omega with a mate.

"I promise you, Gates," I said, running a finger down to one of the other threes. "If something comes up that you need to know, you'll know. But I need you to let me do what Blaze wants without interfering." Another three, this one more recent than even Gates and Kaija's mating. A couple that met at our yearly social event, The Gathering. A couple living the hell Gates dreaded.

He stared at my finger as I trailed down the list. His jaw clenched when I turned the page over, finding another sheet with numbers. All Omegas. All in danger. Almost none with mates.

I watched as his eyes bounced from mine to my finger, the numbers on the page too hard to resist.

"There are more shewolves at stake than just Kaija," I said, my voice quiet but firm. "And the majority" —I tapped another three, the only one on that particular sheet— "don't have a mate to help keep them safe. You're her ally, and I'm yours. Trust in that."

"Yeah...okay." He glanced at the papers again, his brow pulling together. "Guess I should be glad for that mating bond, right?"

I couldn't speak, could barely breathe as I stared at a number on the page. The one for the newly mated couple. The one with the missing Omega and the mate without a clue where she was. The biggest secret in all the pages and the case I'd been busting my ass—and my face—on for weeks.

Gates gave me a backslap goodbye as my stomach sank to my toes. I definitely couldn't tell him about that case. It was more of a secret than the others because of how the kidnappers had been able to get around the mating bond. When a mated pair exchanged blood through bites, they ended up linked somehow. The magic behind it was beyond my knowledgebase, but the fact was a mated shifter could sense or feel where his mate was at all times. Until this last kidnapping when the Omega simply faded off her mate's radar. He could sense her, but not enough to know which direction she'd been taken, the bond reduced to little more than static. Something we hadn't known was possible.

Once Gates disappeared into the back of the denhouse, I sighed and slumped against the bar. Damn it, I hadn't been prepared for so much so soon. The needs of my denmates hadn't factored into my decision to come back for the charity ride. I'd wanted a few days to clear my head, but after my talk with Gates, I was even more distracted. I had enough on my shoulders without feeling as if Kaija's safety from the bastards who'd already tried to take her once was resting on my shoulders. And yet, it was. It always had been.

Still, as much as it probably would have pissed off Gates, I was secretly grateful Kaija had been targeted. Her kidnapping, even if it was only for a few moments, had kicked off an investigation into a threat against all Omegas. I'd been out ever since, hunting the kidnappers, tracking them down. Fighting to save our girls.

Powerful female shifters, the Omegas were considered a treasure to the wolf shifter breed for the strength they gave to a pack. But someone had been taking them against their will, leaving a pile of unanswered questions in their wake. Hell, whoever was collecting the women had decimated four packs so far, killing every other packmate. Of course, that was another thing we couldn't talk about. Much of the shifter community knew about the second pack that had been wiped out, but the others attacked had been kept quiet. The latest one, though not as successful, had also been buried. Layers upon layers of secrets and lies, all covering up the holes in what the packs thought of as the solid foundation of our world.

"You need anything, Shadow?"

I glanced up, meeting the eyes of Klutch. He'd been the manager of the denhouse for years, and he was the road captain on almost all our rides. He was also too kind, too curious, and too observant to pull one over on. It was time to cut and run.

"Nah, man, but thanks. I'm going to hit the rack for a bit."

I grabbed my papers and headed for the stairs that would take me to my apartment on the second floor. My need for sleep far outweighed my desire to be available for Rebel should he want me to do something. Plus, I had work to get done, rumors to research, and I couldn't do all that with the other guys around. Not with the shit I'd have to say.

As soon as I stepped through the doorway into the place I

called home, the picture of my mother caught my attention. Short and dark, she sat among a group of tigers at the edge of a forest. Last I'd heard, she was somewhere in Malaysia living with two other tiger shifter females. Of course, unlike wolves, tigers weren't really pack animals, so what she was doing with those two ladies was probably something I didn't want to think about. Still, she looked happy surrounded by the members of her streak. At ease. Something I envied her for.

Sighing, I slouched off to the bedroom, shucking my clothes along the way and grabbing my favorite ratty sweat pants. I pulled them on quickly, my eyes sticking for a moment at the subtle striping in my groin. Short, thick bands of skin barely a shade darker than the rest crept diagonally from hip to upper thigh in four stripes. Tiger stripes. A birthmark stamped into my skin, subtle and light. Something I'd been fighting to hide most of my life. A secret that, if found out, could get me kicked out of the Feral Breed not by the leadership, but by the guys who fought beside me as brothers.

My unique heritage had been both a blessing and a curse. My tiger side was both terrifying and strong, a better hunter than most wolves, sneaky as all fuck, and one hell of a vicious fighter when called upon, even if I remained in my wolf or human form. But my mixed background had gotten me kicked out of packs and shunned by most wolves when I was younger, so I hid it. Tucked that secret way down deep and left it to rot.

Blaze and Rebel were the only ones who knew about my mother's breed and how that affected my abilities. Both men understood the impact the added genetic material had on my inner wolf as well as the way other wolf shifters would treat me if they knew. We'd all heard it and seen it before: the isolation, the disgust, the way the judgmental would spit out that ultimate insult...*mutt*. But Blaze and Rebel had accepted me, allowed me to prospect for the Feral Breed and let me earn my colors without bias or hate. Most importantly, they helped me hide the truth from others who wouldn't be so accepting. Blaze's mate, Dante, had a similar genetic makeup, though coming from his father's side and several generations back. Blaze was well-versed in our mixed-up bloodlines, our dual animal natures, and he took full advantage of it.

Blaze had requested my presence in Chicago to help track down the missing women not long after the incident with Kaija. At the time, we'd only been aware of three shewolves involved. But the longer we searched, the more truth came to light, and the more women seemed to have been taken. Seemed, because some packs refused to tell us if the women were Omegas or not. Others had simply disappeared. But as word spread of the danger brewing around the Omegas, the stories began rolling in, other packs too afraid of losing a beloved packmate not to tell someone when things seemed unusual in their area.

My job—my mission, my duty to the breed—was to find what had somehow become the unfindable. Nothing could get in my way of that. Not the fear of having my tiger side revealed, not the risk of being shunned by my Feral Breed brothers for being a mutt. Nothing could get in my way of solving this mystery and returning the Omegas to their packs.

Because every time I looked at those numbers on the page, it was Kaija's face I saw, and it was the memory of Gates' pain-filled roar as his mate was taken right in front of his eyes that played through my mind. A sound that haunted me even in my dreams.

TWO

Scarlett

THE MUSIC THUMPED THROUGH the speakers, making the dance floor vibrate with the level of bass. I smiled at the man dancing in front of me. He stepped closer, watching as I swung my hips and turned, as I gave myself over to the music and the energy of the club. To the heat of the place and the people filling it. I liked this, liked his eyes on me, liked the steamy looks he sent me. I liked being the center of attention, even if I didn't like him all that much.

Doug worked at the bank down the street from the house my sister and I rented. Nice guy, good-looking in a very bland sort of way, but my God, was he dull. He'd spent dinner talking about some kind of dog his parents own. An entire meal discussing dogs...*please*. I preferred the company of cats, and I made sure he knew it. He hadn't known what to say at that point. Of course, I hadn't used the word cats. I'd been a bit crasser than that, something he hadn't seemed impressed with. Not that I cared all that much what he thought about my language and my innuendos. He was a distraction—nothing more, nothing less.

Even after the awkward dinner discussing dogs and not

discussing pussies, we ended up at the bar around the corner
from where I used to live. Being back in this neighborhood put
me on edge, so I'd been drinking and dancing and flirting more
than I usually would. Letting myself lose a bit of control with
every song, every drink, every smile. Avoiding the possibility of
the whos—or whats—could come walking through that door.

Knowing there were men who could turn into wolves
hanging out just a block away tended to make me a bit…
anxious.

I glanced around the room as I spun, my long hair fanning
out around me. The move was easy to pull off as part of my
dance, but it was more of an investigative procedure. Out of
control or not, I needed to search the bar, to look for that
telltale black leather jacket or vest the guys wore. To know if
I had more time to enjoy myself or if I needed to head for the
door. This was Feral Breed territory, and I was more than happy
to keep avoiding that group.

Seeing no sign of motorcycle club leathers, I gave myself
back over to the beat. Spinning around, I smiled and pulled
Doug closer by the belt loop at his hip. He had that fiery
look in his eye as he watched, the one that said he wanted to
maybe take this someplace quiet. Someplace more private. And
though Doug was a dull boy and not at all the type of guy I'd
usually go out with more than once, I was almost considering
it. Almost…but not quite. The reality was, Doug would never
be the guy for me. Not forever. But for right now…

Doug pulled me closer, his hand sliding over my hip and
down my ass. *All* the way down my ass. I pressed closer, catching
his eye and smirking. The guy had moves, that was for sure. All
night he'd been giving me sexy little touches, small teases that
made me burn for more. And this one was no different. He had
me riding a knife-edge of desire, one that made me want to fall.
Or maybe it wasn't him… Maybe it was something in the air.
Some kind of magick dancing on the night winds.

Leering, lips turned up in a half smile, he squeezed my cheek harder, his fingers brushing between my legs. I wobbled on my six-inch heels, catching my breath as he pressed deep into my flesh. So demanding, not something I usually liked. But this time, I could deal. At least for a few more songs. At least until he made me feel human again.

Doug pulled me into his arms, pressing his erection into my belly and nuzzling my neck before bringing his lips to my ear.

"Scarlett letter," he said, the joke on my name and the smell of the beer on his breath making my nose crinkle. "Want to go back to my place?"

I inched back and smiled, running my hands down his chest and swiveling my hips against him. "Either I'm not that easy or you're not that suave. I think I'll keep dancing for now."

Rolling his eyes and giving me a patronizing smile that stoked my temper and made me want to knee him in the balls, he grabbed my hand and pulled me all the way against him. "Whatever the lady wants, she gets. Though the offer's still on the table." He shuffled back, a lazy smile on his face, a certainty in his eyes that made me itch. "I'll get you another drink."

I nodded, shooing him toward the bar with a plastic smile. That expression fell the second he turned away, though. Something had my knickers in a twist, had me horny and cranky and altogether uncomfortable in my own skin. Whether it was being close to the Feral Breed denhouse that I'd avoided like the plague since moving to this city or it was something about Dull Doug, I couldn't tell. But my mood was quickly going from tipsy and flirty to ballbuster-Betty..

Shaking off the sense of irritation simmering in my gut, I danced my way across the floor and back into the crowd. Damn, it felt good to let loose and just…be. To forget about futures and fate and the reality of being a witch without a coven for one night. I needed this date, even if I was putting up with

Doug the dull banker. Dull and pushy, but not all bad. He had enough heat packing in those overly-expensive-made-to-look-casually-worn jeans to keep a girl's attention. With the way he kept pressing himself against me, it was impossible not to take notice. Dull Doug with the big dick. And a demanding personality. Only one of those three being an attribute I found appealing.

When Doug found me in the middle of a throng of dancers, beer and whiskey in hand, I was ninety percent sure he was trying to picture me naked. The look on his face, the leer, as if anything physical between us was a sure thing. When he smiled and handed me a glass with a lime on the edge, glancing down the top of my dress as he did, that percentage inched up to ninety-four.

I grabbed my drink and took a sip, still moving to the beat of the DJ, keeping my eyes on the people around us. Gyrating bodies crowded the floor, sensual movements between singles and couples, writhing and stroking and giving it all up to the music. The temperature in the press of bodies rose with every beat, crept up with every refrain. Heat and lust and desire pulsed with the beat of the music, sexy lyrics making people brave. Making them wanton. And Doug, darling dull Doug with the big dick and the sense of entitlement when it came to my affection, was looking at me as if I was some kind of wet dream.

Ninety-eight percent.

Brushing off my unease, I let him move closer, let him press himself against me once more. I held my ground even as some instinct made me want to flinch away from his touch. His cheeks flushed, his eyes darkened, and he gave me a look that played out every little dirty detail racing through his mind. I knew what he wanted before he made his move, before he spoke a word. Felt the storm between us brew before the first rumble of thunder. Knew that, to him, it was time to get a little sweaty and a lot naked.

Doug yanked me closer, his touch a little rougher than I would have preferred. "C'mon, baby. Let's go to my place and get away from this crowd."

And there it was…the non-question. The order to do what he wanted instead of what I did. The demand. I shook my head and backed away, untangling myself from his arms. He followed, both hands reaching for my hips, my ass, my thighs. Grabby.

"Doug, stop." I put my hand against his chest, calling upon the power of my sacred element, upon the fire magick that always lived within me, to be ready. Just in case. "I don't want to leave right now."

He rolled his eyes and drank his beer, looking over the crowd. I sighed and tried to focus on the music, on the beat, but it was no use. My mood had sunk straight past ballbuster to Lorena Bobbitt. Why did he have to try to order me around? Did he think he owned me because I let him buy me dinner after three weeks of him chasing me every chance he could? He'd gone from Dull Doug to Dull Dictator Doug in a single sentence, and I didn't like that transition.

I'd spent enough time dealing with people trying to tell me what to do.

"I think maybe we should call it a night." I stepped back, pissed off, sparks firing under my skin. Fuck, my magick was all kinds of screwed up. Had been for months, since we'd driven away from the coven who'd claimed to be family. Since I'd refused to do anything more than handle my elemental fire and had lost the balance powers like mine needed.

"If we have to dance, then I'll dance." Doug grabbed my arm again and pulled, this time making me lose my balance. Smirking as if he liked showing me how easily he could boss me around. "I'm not really into this kind of music, Scarlett, so let's get this over with."

The glass I'd been holding shattered on the dance floor, barely audible over the music, hardly a whisper, but it screamed in my head. The memories of someone else saying Doug's words stealing my breath.

"Let's get this over with. I hereby ask the coven to initiate a shunning."

Someone who'd been demanding and drunk on her power. Someone I'd grown up with, who'd betrayed me and my sisters.

"Our coven is being hunted, and yet she goes to the ones who would kill us all. She cavorts with them. She spreads her legs for them."

Someone who'd kicked us out of our own coven, our home, and left us to dangle in the wind.

"Hey, what's wrong?" Doug asked as I took two steps back.

"I need to go home." My voice came out as a croak, pictures from the night Bethesda Marrin banished my sister from our coven, our home, flooding my mind and bringing back all those emotions. The pain, the heartbreak, the sense of desolation. The rage.

The complete and utter lack of control over my own life.

Doug's eyebrows dropped and he frowned. "What? No, stay. I said I'd dance with you."

I shook my head, my stomach turning as the past overlapped my present.

"The decision has been made. Pack your belongings."

"I can't." The dance floor spun and the lights blazed against my skin. Burning me. Burning everything. My magick setting me on fire from the inside out. I closed my eyes for a moment, blocking the stimuli of the club before taking a deep breath and giving Doug my best fake smile. "I need to leave. I'm not feeling well."

Doug didn't look convinced. "You sure you don't want another drink or something?"

I put one hand up and sidestepped him. "No, I'm good."

"Scarlett" —he grabbed my elbow, spinning me around to face him— "I get it, you want to go. Let me take you home. I promise to leave you safe and sound at the door."

Tired of arguing and fighting back a horrible wave of nausea, I let him lead me through the bar and outside. The storm in my mind blew strong and loud, too much to allow me time to look around. To notice if anyone was wearing the leather coats I'd been so worried about earlier. My biggest fear reduced to barely a whisper of thought as my past set off a firestorm in my mind.

The wind blew in from the west as we stepped outside, but otherwise the night was quiet and comfortable. Late spring in Detroit was a good time of year. Warm but not yet humid. A time for rebirth and sowing seeds of future promises, for sex and love and a fresh outlook on life. But not for me, especially not tonight.

A tense and awkward car ride later, Doug dropped me at my door. Our goodbye consisted of little more than a kiss to my forehead and a declaration that he'd call. Not that I expected him to or that I'd be too excited if he did. The night had been a ridiculous disaster. I saw no reason to try for a second date.

Once inside the house I shared with my sister, I hurried up the stairs to the bathroom. The place was nice if not a little small, situated in an old neighborhood right on the Detroit River. Very…suburban and family-friendly. I'd liked living downtown in Beast's townhouse, but that hadn't worked out. My sister, Amber, the future-teller of our crazy clan, had seen a vision of him kicking her out, so she'd packed up and left. I'd followed her because, while this town may have been a bit too Cleaver Family for me, living here kept my family together. I'd walked away from my coven to support one sister; I clung to them both now. Amber and I were missing our sister Zuri to complete the Weaver triplets, but she lived just two towns over. Across the bridge on a little island town south of Detroit. An almost perfect spot for a water witch like her.

But too far away to keep our tiny coven together, thus making our inner magick fade, our powers too much to handle alone.

Witches by blood, we had left our hometown behind to follow Zuri and her red thread to Detroit. Phoenix, my soon-to-be brother-in-law, called Zuri his mate, but I guessed that's what you got when the Fates declared your soul mate was an animal. Well, part of the time. Wolf shifters rarely seemed to stay in their doggy form for long. They tended to go human, the ones we knew donning leather vests and jackets and riding motorcycles around town as if they didn't shift into an animal at will. As if they were normal...not that I knew exactly what normal was.

I was washing my face when Amber slipped in, arms crossed and wearing one hell of a frown.

"Don't bother." I grabbed my toothbrush and toothpaste. "I don't need your lecture."

"You know it's going to happen."

"Screw you," I said around a mouthful of toothpaste foam. "It's not going to happen if I don't want it to. And I don't."

"Really? Okay, keep telling yourself that. But remember, I'm the one with the power of precognition, and I say there's no way around it."

I spit, turning on the faucet to wash down the blue bubbles, avoiding her eyes. "You're wrong. We walked away from everything we knew to not have someone rule us. I'm not about to go back into some kind of dysfunctional relationship with a man I've never met."

"I'm not wrong, and he's your red thread. Your soul mate."

"Fuck that." Tossing my towel on the counter, I shoved past her, desperate to get away. "You don't know everything, Magic Eight Ball."

"Scarlett—"

"No." I spun, anger making my fingers burn as my beloved fire element reacted to my emotions. "No one gets to tell me how to run my life. Not you, not Zuri, not our former coven, and sure as hell not some crazy blip of the Fates you keep claiming to see. This is my life, all mine, and I'm going to run it the way I choose."

Stomach roiling, I rushed back into the bathroom, barely making it to the toilet before the dinner and the alcohol made a reappearance. The acid burned my throat and made my nose run, but I welcomed it. Better to hurt physically than to feel that unbreakable noose of betrayal wrapped around my neck for a moment longer. Let it burn... I could handle any pain after the night of Zuri's banishment.

Amber grabbed my long hair and held it up as she placed a cool washcloth against the back of my neck. Always the little mother. Always the one cleaning up the messes Zuri and I made. But not this time.

"I won't let something as ridiculous as a vision make my choices," I cried, spitting out the last of the sick.

Amber shushed me and pulled my bangs off my forehead. "It's fated, Scar. I've tried to look past it every way I know how, but there is no past it. Your future is decided and unavoidable. You'll succumb to it eventually."

"Never." I pushed to my feet and hurried to the sink to rinse out my mouth once more. "I will never let the Fates decide who I'm supposed to fall in love with and spend the rest of my life chasing after."

I rushed out the door and down the hall, desperate for the safety and privacy of my room. "I make my own choices, Amber."

Long, dark hair in a high ponytail, Amber shook her head, a frown on her face.

"Not this time, Scar. There is no choice."

THREE

Shadow

I PULLED UP OUTSIDE Phoenix's cottage on the river early one cool morning. A light fog hung in the air, giving the place an ethereal glow. From the clean stone front to the flowers in the window boxes to the freshly painted trim, the place looked like it belonged in some English countryside or fairy tale. It felt like more than a house, exuding a sense of warmth, of home. An odd twist of pain shot through my chest and my wolf whined. This was what he wanted—to pair up, find the mate meant for us, and create our own tiny pack. I rubbed a thumb over that little ache and shook off my wolf's sudden sense of loneliness. We had work to get done, and thinking about things that probably weren't meant to be wasn't going to make that work go any faster.

Sliding off my bike, I hooked my helmet over the handlebar and took a deep breath before heading for the front door. Phoenix had been working on updating the old cottage for a couple of months from what I understood, the shifter in a mad rush to ready his den before his mate had their baby. When he called last night to ask if I could help him lay wood flooring, I said yes. It was the least I could do to help my denmate out.

Plus, I hadn't spent much time with him since he'd earned his patch. I wanted to correct that.

Phoenix's mate Zuri opened the door before I could knock, a big smile on her face and a red T-shirt stretched across her ball-shaped belly.

"Morning, Shadow. Would you like a cup of coffee?"

"No, but thank you." As soon as I stepped inside, the hair on the back of my neck stood up. I sniffed again and again, trying not to look as if I was ignoring Zuri. She continued to make small talk, oblivious to my sudden need to shift to an animal form and stalk through her home hunting that scent. Faded but not old, the captivating aroma wasn't one from Zuri or Phoenix. It was unique, something I'd never noticed before. Something I wanted more of.

Both my inner beasts prowled closer to the surface of my mind, ready to burst through and take over. The whirlwind of growls and snarls inside my head quickly became overwhelming. Standing stock-still in the living room, I locked my jaw and fought against my own mind, the man in me afraid to move, worried about upsetting the precarious balance and shifting. If my wolf won, Zuri would probably be okay seeing as she was mated to a wolf shifter. If my tiger won... Well, there would be no unlicking that stamp. He couldn't win. Period.

"Are you sure I can't get you anything?"

I swallowed hard and shook my head, wishing she would stop talking. I needed to concentrate. The witch had done nothing wrong, but something in the house was making me lose control.

With strength of will born from decades of hiding what I was, I pushed both beasts into the corners of my mind. They didn't go willingly, but I refused to let them win. After a moment, the push grew easier, the human side of me no longer having to fight to stay in control. The tiger almost disappeared, hiding as always in the far reaches, waiting for his turn to come out and rule. The wolf relinquished control, but he stayed closer to the forefront. Watching. Waiting. For what, I had no idea. But not ready to let go completely.

"Why do they call you Shadow?" Zuri asked, watching me, smiling. One hand on her pregnant belly. Making me dig deeper for control.

I took a deep breath to banish the residual shakiness I felt inside. "I'm fast, and I tend to sneak up on people. When I'm working, I can usually get in and out of places unnoticed."

"Huh," she said, her brow furrowed. "I would have figured you'd be called Doc, since you're a doc and all."

"Too obvious." I shook my head, my nerves finally settling, my heart rate calming. "Besides, I don't practice medicine and haven't for a long time. I'm a glorified field medic at this point."

Zuri nodded and chatted on about something to do with medicinal herbs, but I was stuck in my head. Fuck me, that had been close. Oddly so. I hadn't had such a difficult time controlling myself since I was a teenager just learning how to balance the beasts within. And I still had no idea what caused the reaction.

"Hey, brother." Phoenix came walking down the stairs, barefoot and wearing only a pair of sweat pants. The dick. It was ass-crack early o'clock and I'd already showered, dressed, and driven my ass all the way out to this little island south of the city. Still, I was happy as fuck that he'd appeared. His wolf essence immediately put mine at ease, gave him a sense of pack and togetherness, giving me one less thing to have to fight.

"Good to see you're ready to work, brother."

I laughed when he rolled his eyes, relaxing my shoulders as the scent of shifter overrode everything else around me. I almost wanted that other scent back, the cold heat of it something I suddenly craved, but I didn't want to fight for control all day. This was better, the smell of something familiar keeping me settled.

Phoenix gripped my forearms before bringing me in for a backslap.

"Thanks for coming, man." He took a step back, looking me over in a very Rebelesque way. He must not have seen anything off because he grinned and nodded at Zuri. "I got a late start. My girl kept me up all night."

Zuri snorted a laugh. "Liar. I bought him a new creeper, so he was in the garage half the night putzing with my Yenko."

"Our Yenko." Phoenix smirked and gave me a wink, obviously riling up his mate. I wasn't sure what game he was playing—everyone knew that car was hers. And damn if we all weren't more than a little jealous of that fact. The car was sex on wheels, loud and rough and pure muscle. Every guy at the denhouse got serious gearhead chub just talking about it.

Zuri spun to face her mate, her face angry and her eyes fiery, a hint of wind upsetting the air around us. "Adam Tackett, that is my car. I don't care if we get married. It's my car. I don't care if you want to tinker with it. It's my car. You're allowed to drive it, but it's *my car*."

I chuckled as she advanced on him. While she wasn't as short as Kaija, she still had a man who towered over her. Watching her little, round self berate a shifter the size of Phoenix was entertaining. Knowing she'd win against him simply because of his instincts to protect her at all cost was hilarious.

"Okay, okay," Phoenix said as he grabbed Zuri around her waist and pulled her against his chest. "Your car. Not my car. Never my car. Got it. Now give me a kiss before I take Shadow into the other room to do manly things."

Zuri gave him a solid glare before rising up on the balls of her feet. The two kissed with more passion than was probably appropriate considering they weren't alone, so I left them to it and strolled deeper into the living room.

Four new bookcases sat against the wall, two on each side of the fireplace, capturing my attention. Phoenix had mentioned he'd built them himself and I had to admit, he'd done a nice job. Tall, wide, with moulding applied to the top and bottom, they looked as if they'd been standing in their spots since the day the house was built.

The couple had packed each shelf full of books and pictures and trinkets, making every section unique. On one shelf, the dominating decoration was a large picture of three women in front of a lighthouse. Zuri stood in the middle, her arms around the other two, a huge grin on their faces. She was one of a set of triplets, so the other two were probably her sisters, though I had yet to meet them.

All three women were exceptionally pretty with their dark hair and big eyes. But they were witches, a fact that worried me. Witches and wolves didn't normally mix, though apparently the Fates hadn't been informed of that fact seeing as they'd paired Zuri with Phoenix. The regional head of the NALB and pack Alphas had to be up in arms over their mating, if they knew. When those old windbags got word of a baby being born from the union, their heads would probably spin. Another secret to file away, as I certainly wouldn't want to bring any attention to the couple.

"Off you two go," Zuri said with a chuckle, interrupting my rambling thoughts. I turned to find her batting Phoenix away, her smile wide and her cheeks flushed. Phoenix grinned, his hands grabbing at her hips. The two were obviously happy, mated, and in love… A trifecta they won the second they met. Phoenix deserved that win, having started his shifter life in violence. He'd earned a little happiness, no matter who brought it to him.

Once the two finally let each other go, I followed Phoenix to the stacks of wood planks just over the threshold of the kitchen. The house wasn't all that large, but installing wood flooring, even in a small space, could take a lot of time. Hopefully with the two of us, it wouldn't take more than a day or two to finish the lower level. I had the time as I waited to find another lead on the Omega case. To get word on the next place to go or person to question.

"Amber and Scarlett are coming to pick me up in about an hour," Zuri said as she headed for the stairs. "Please, no hard rock blaring until I leave, okay?"

"Wouldn't dream of it," Phoenix replied. He gave me a shrug. "Gives her a headache."

"Understood."

The two of us set to work, laying out the planks along one wall before filling in across the room. Saws, mumbled measurements, and the sound of knee hammers firing filled the space with enough noise to not need the blasting music, though Phoenix kept a radio playing from the bookcases. Zuri brought out a pitcher of lemonade and a couple of glasses at one point while we nudged and hammered the wood into place.

"Damn it," Phoenix growled, interrupting my concentration as I measured a plank.

"What's up?"

He tossed his rubber mallet across the room and growled. "Fucking walls are completely out of square."

I shrugged. "That's part of the charm of such an old house. Imperfect walls and corners."

"Yeah, well, I'm pretty sure you're even older than this place. You got imperfect angles, too?" He ran a hand through his hair, a frustrated smile on his face.

I paused, though, fighting not to duck my head and curl my shoulders. His words hit home in a way he hadn't intended them, made me feel suddenly less than able. Imperfect corners didn't begin to describe all the things wrong with me.

Shaking off as much of the odd melancholy as I could, I went back to my tape measure. "I'm sure I do, man."

As the whine of the saw died down, a car pulled up outside, the engine loud and rough.

"Shit," Phoenix said, glancing toward the front window. "The Weaver clan is reunited."

"Zuri's sisters?"

"That's right, you've never met them, have you?"

I shook my head. "Can't say that I have."

Phoenix stood and cracked his neck. "C'mon, I'll introduce you while we grab a drink. I need to stretch before we hit it again."

"Sure." I followed Phoenix out of the dining room, brushing the sawdust off my jeans as I went.

"I really do appreciate you helping me out, man," Phoenix said as we headed toward the entryway.

"Anytime. You know that." I had barely finished my words when the front door swung open. Two women strolled in, laughing loud and bright, stealing every ounce of my attention. The first one froze when she saw me, staring, going pale. Her green eyes went wide and unfocused, almost staring through me as she gasped and stumbled, knocking against the wall. I lurched toward her, hoping to catch her before she fell, but pulled up short as the second woman caught my eye.

Short, curvy, with tan skin and streaks of fire in her hair, she made an aura of color explode in my mind by simply existing. Heart racing, dick as hard as granite, I locked eyes on her and stared. Soft and feminine without appearing weak, beautiful without that air of arrogance some women carried, she practically radiated confidence. So attractive, so sexy, so fucking perfect.

Without looking my way, she grabbed her sister's arm, pulling her back to her feet. "Damn, Amber. Walk much?"

Before I could say or do anything, her eyes met mine in a moment that rocked the very foundation of my soul. Time stopped. Froze. Ended. Such deep, striking eyes. My entire world shrank down to nothing but the green of those eyes. To the shock of finding her, the pull of my soul to hers. *Holy shit...*

The wolf side of me howled in delight, knowing he'd finally found his mate. But the other...the other growled, interested but wary. The witch power sitting beneath my mate's skin incited fear where there should only be want. Still, if the desperate need I felt to wrap myself around her was any indication, the little witch was to be mine. According to the Fates and my wolf within, at least. My other half, my fated one. My mate.

Words. Phoenix was saying words, but I couldn't pay attention. All I saw was her, all I knew was her. I tried to smile and approach, wanting to officially meet the woman who was to be my mate, but those green eyes shot sparks of anger and fear as I did.

"No," she said with force, the syllable breaking through the mating haze her presence had wrapped around me. Like a movie, everything came back into focus. The room, the people, the words. And my mate, looking right at me...refusing me.

"No what, Sparkles?" Phoenix laughed, not understanding. Not knowing. But how could he? All she'd said was...

"No." A whisper this time, quiet but firm, eyes still locked on mine. One word. My mate said only one word and my entire world collapsed.

"Scarlett." The other sister looked from one of us to the other, concern clear in her expression.

"I said no." Scarlett, my fated mate, set my heart aflame as she refused our bond without knowing anything about me, leaving nothing but ash. Fear and anxiety rolled off her, and those big green eyes suddenly darted to look anywhere but at me. Fiery dragon to frightened mouse in an instant. "I'll wait in the car."

Scarlett rushed out the door, not even glancing back in my direction. Amber stared after her for a moment before turning on me. Watching. Inspecting. Knowing. I raised an eyebrow in challenge, but she ignored me, instead frowning as she turned for the stairs.

"I'll grab Zuri," she said, disappearing to the second floor.

"What the hell was all that about?" Phoenix asked, his brow pulled down in confusion.

I shrugged, battling the tsunami of emotion inside of me while doing my best to keep my face and body language calm. I wouldn't let Phoenix know his future sister-in-law had just ripped my heart out with a single word and stomped all over the possibility of a future with me. No sense in adding friction to our relationship or between him and Scarlett. Their bond was permanent, the link of siblings and fated mates something I doubted could be broken. I was the odd man out, and this was just one more secret to add to my pile. One more lie to have to remember.

"No clue. Let's get back to work, yeah? The floor's not going to lay itself."

FOUR

Scarlett

MY HANDS SHOOK AND liquid fire raced through my veins as I gripped the steering wheel of my car. Of all the fucking luck. For months...*months!*...I'd avoided interacting with Phoenix's denmates. Amber had seen the red thread tied to my heart leading into that damn denhouse, so I'd kept my distance. I knew one of those animalistic jerks would end up trying to tie me down for eternity. Not that I would let them.

How could the Fates be so wrong? Didn't my opinion matter at all? How ridiculous was it to be tied to someone you'd never met, forced into some kind of voodooed-up relationship because that one person just happened to be...something. Something the Fates were allowed to decide was right for you, as if you couldn't decide for yourself. Well, the Fates could take a giant fucking walk off a tiny little cliff for all I cared. I would not be forced into some relationship I didn't choose. Not me. Let my sister carry on the line of witches and dogs. I wanted no part of it. No matter how much my heart hurt when I turned my back on that man.

I jumped when the doors opened, having been too far lost in my own thoughts to see my sisters walk out of the house. A pregnant Zuri plopped into the front seat next to me as Amber slid in the back, one sister oblivious, one definitely not.

"What just happened?" Zuri asked. "And why does it smell like smoke in here?"

I shrugged, ignoring the truth screaming inside my head. "Nothing. Why?"

Zuri rolled her eyes. "Uh, because I heard you run out of there like something was chasing you. And it literally smells like smoke in your car."

"I always smell like smoke." I caught Amber's eye in the rearview mirror. Hard eyes, maybe even a little sad. Well, screw that. I didn't need her pity or her anger. I glared right back, daring her to open her mouth. She pursed her lips and turned to look out the window, though the victory only left a hollow feeling in the pit of my stomach.

Turning the car around to head back toward the road, I shook my head and lied to my sister, something I'd never really done before. "I left so I didn't get a headache. The smell from the new floor was getting to me."

"It looks good, right?" Zuri asked, chipper and smiling. Completely oblivious to the giant, gaping holes riddled with guilt and shame forming inside my mind. "I'm just glad Shadow was able to come over and help. Phoenix can't do that whole place by himself. He was going to ask Beast, but with the baby and all, he figured they needed some time as a family."

I hummed, stuck on the fact that the man who would try to lord over my destiny was named Shadow. How very fitting. Shadows were made of darkness. They lived in creepy corners and dank basements. Shadows were the opposite of what I wanted or who I was. As a fire witch, I could light up the sky so bright, every shadow around me would be banished forever. And that's what I needed to do…burn my end of the thread connecting us until there was nothing but ash left.

I would not be some dog's little bitch just because the Fates said I should be.

Even if the look of pain that flashed across his face when I refused him would probably haunt me for the rest of my life.

THE MUSIC BLARED, SHAKING the nearly-deserted dance floor. Most bars tended to be a little empty so early in the evening, but I hadn't wanted to wait. Not after the day I'd had. The thread connecting me to Shadow had pulled and squeezed all afternoon while I'd been with my sisters. It suffocated me. Made me want to rage against its hold.

Even now, hours after meeting the dog, I could still feel the weight of his stare on my skin. The sensation drove me crazy, making me anxious and angry. A bad combination for a woman who tended to set things on fire when she got emotional. So I'd convinced the girls to head to the bar after our shopping trip. I needed a few drinks and a little time on the dance floor. I needed to surrender to the DJ as I fought off Shadow's leash.

Amber and Zuri sat in a booth with Charlotte across the room. Charlotte was mated to the president of the Feral Breed den, another woman who ended up giving away her freedom to a trick of Fate. She was fully leashed—bite marks and all—though not yet pregnant if the dark beer she appeared to be drinking was any indication. The three laughed and chatted, but I didn't have a single care to join them. I wanted to dance, to have the music take me someplace else. To let loose and find my freedom. To just be alone for a while.

"Hey there, beautiful."

And just like that, my happy little bubble burst. I did my best to smile as Dull Doug walked over, but it was a struggle. To be honest, I was happier to see the two glasses in his hands than him, and I was not a big drinker.

"Hey, stranger," I said once he was close enough to hear me. "Stalking me?"

He shrugged, attempting to look casual but not pulling it off very well.

"Just out with a few friends from work. I saw you dancing alone and thought you might be a little thirsty." He held out a glass. "Jack and diet with a lime, right?"

I smiled my first real smile since I'd left Zuri's house that morning after meeting...him. This was what I needed: liquor, dancing, and the possibility of a little untangled entanglement of the physical variety.

Biting back the sick feeling that thought gave me, I plastered on a grin. "You're kind of my savior right now."

He smiled when I took the drink from his hand. A bright, wide smile that made his eyes turn up at the corners. A real smile. Not one brought on because the Fates *wanted* him to smile at a particular someone or because some wacky need to reproduce forced him to. Doug may have been dull, but he was real. His feelings for me were real, whatever they might have been. And that was something I couldn't ignore. Doug might demand, but he'd never be able to control me the way a red thread could. Never be able to hurt me...because he'd just never mean that much to me. Doug was safe.

I danced closer, downing my drink and letting my body brush his. "Dance with me."

He smirked and placed both glasses on a nearby table before pulling me close. His hands gripped my hips, strong and rough. I let him yank on me, let him slide his knee between my legs as I pushed my breasts against his chest. I let him take.

Just as I was getting into the moment, as Doug's hands slid from my hips to cup my ass, I felt a tug on my chest, a need to look toward the table where my sisters sat. A desire to...

Oh, hell no.

Phoenix, Shadow, and Charlotte's mate, Rebel, sat with the girls. All six of them talking and laughing. The scene made my stomach clench, but I couldn't look away. Shadow, wearing his long, dark hair in a low ponytail, sat next to Amber. He didn't seem to be saying much, more listening as the others spoke. Attentive.

I wanted to ignore him, to forget he was there and get back to dancing with Dull Doug, but Shadow hijacked my senses. I could feel him, see him, practically smell him on the air. If he'd speak, I was sure I could hear him from across the room and over the loud music. By the Goddess, the draw to him, the need to move closer, was burning. Physically painful. And I hated him for it.

He looked my way, a small glance, but one that filled me with a sense of longing so strong, I almost headed straight for him. My thread pulled tight, my heart on fire, the desire to touch and taste almost too strong to resist.

Almost, but not quite.

Growing more pissed off by the second, I wrapped my arms around Doug's neck and gyrated my hips with his. Let Shadow sit and watch me. I'd definitely give him a show. As I expected, Doug bent down, running his nose along the side of my face until he was breathing all loud and humid in my ear.

Sounding like a pig grunting.

"You are so beautiful."

I kept my fake smile in place and twisted in his hold, rubbing my ass against him as his arms came around to squeeze me close. Ugh, something about being with him felt so wrong. So awkward and uncomfortable. Maybe if I just closed my eyes, I could pretend it wasn't Dull Doug rubbing his probably dull dick against my ass like a high school kid at his first homecoming dance. Maybe I could picture myself with someone more my speed…a little wild, a little crazy, a whole lot sexy without being an arrogant douchenozzle.

As soon as the first image of Shadow appeared in my mind, my eyes popped open and my stomach revolted. *Fuck* and *no*. Not happening. Who cared that he was about ten levels of hot with his light, almond-shaped eyes and his dark, shiny hair? As if the fact that he was tall—way taller than Dull Doug— and obviously strong enough to toss me around if he chose to, was a reason to feel attraction to him. Fine, he was handsome with his ridiculous cheekbones, full lips, and smoke-gray eyes, but that wasn't the only thing I wanted. That wasn't what kept drawing my gaze to the table, to him, to the bulging muscles in his arms and the long, thick lines of his thighs.

Shit.

I danced with my eyes closed until the sick feeling in my gut became too strong. Until I couldn't fight any longer. Needing a break, I pulled out of Doug's hold, put some space between us. My stomach twisted and the rope around my heart tightened, dragging me down, making me dizzy with the pressure.

"I'm going to run to the ladies' room."

Doug shrugged, backing away, presumably to meet up with his coworkers. I spun and hurried for the stairs leading to the basement bathrooms, too afraid of seeing Shadow watching me to even glance at the table where he'd been sitting. I couldn't see those eyes again, couldn't resist the pull of their gaze.

Grabbing the handrail, I ran down the concrete steps that would lead me to the privacy I desperately needed. I made it to the second to last stair before my ankle turned, my hand slipping on the metal rail and my arms flailing as I stumbled forward. I had one sickening moment of mentally screaming oh-my-Goddess-I'm-falling before a strong hand grabbed my elbow, keeping me from face-planting on the concrete. A hand that felt as familiar as the fire that wrapped around me, that burned and licked and brought happiness and balance to my soul, more than I'd ever known. One hand, one touch. Only one person it could belong to.

I yanked my arm out of Shadow's hold, stumbling backward. My face burned, my pride a little knocked down from almost falling in front of him, but that didn't help my temper.

"You don't need to follow me, you know."

Shadow furrowed his brow, his forehead going all squished and lined and kind of adorable. Those unusual eyes of his focused right on my face. The hard lines of his body too close not to notice. To crave.

He had to be such an asshole to be so pretty.

"I was down here first."

"What? No. You were at the table with my sisters." I pointed up, only just taking into account the fact that Shadow stood facing the opposite way I had been headed, as if he'd been coming up the stairs as I'd been going down them. "Oh."

"Yeah, oh." He shook his head and bounded up the stairs two at a time. "The words you're looking for are 'thank' and 'you,' by the way."

I stood there, mouth literally hanging open as I watched him disappear around the turn. The jerk. He didn't look back, leaving me behind as if I were nothing. As if I weren't the woman the Fates had decided would be perfect for him. As if he didn't feel the same connection to me that I did to him.

Not that I wanted him to.

FIVE

Shadow

THE LINGERING BITTERNESS OF regret and frustration from the way I'd run up the stairs the night before had me rolling out of bed earlier than normal. Damn but Scarlett had walls. Huge, nonscalable walls with defenses that could cut a man to the quick in an instant. Walls that left me feeling like a failure and a coward for refusing to tear them down with my fists. Scarlett wasn't the type of girl you pushed into anything, though. She needed to be wooed, to be enticed. She needed to make her own decisions. I just wished her decisions included giving me a fucking chance.

Back sore and dick hard, I stumbled into the bathroom, resigned to start my day…sans plan to win over my mate. I brushed my teeth while glaring at the erection that refused to go down. Fucker had been hard all night, waking me up to jerk off more times than I cared to admit. All because of a woman I couldn't have. If I didn't stop obsessing over Scarlett Weaver, I was going to suffer some serious chafing.

It'd been less than twenty-four hours since I first saw her, since she refused me on sight, and yet I couldn't get her off my mind. That sexy hair, the mouth-watering curves, those jade eyes that about peered right through me. The lilt in her voice, the kindness in her eyes when she looked at her sisters. My every thought centered on her, my every need overshadowed by my desire for her. But being close to me was quite obviously the last thing she wanted…most of the time. Except when I touched her and her breath caught, or I looked at her and found her staring at me. Or when I felt the tug of our bond around my heart, indicating that, while she'd spoken her refusal, she hadn't truly accepted it yet.

She was driving me mad.

Unfortunately, that was mad as in crazy and mad as in pissed at the same time. The way she let that guy hang all over her at the bar was such an infuriatingly immature move. Deep down, I knew she only did it because I was there, watching her, but man, did that cut sting. It'd been hard for me to sit with everyone else and watch the woman who was supposed to be my mate rub her round ass on some other guy's junk as her eyes kept flitting my way. I'd been ready to shift right there in the bar, had felt an almost irresistible need to protect what was mine.

But the last thing Scarlett Weaver could be called was mine. She'd refused me outright. And though I felt the bond between us, and saw the desire in her eyes, she obviously had no interest in pursuing anything to do with me. A fact that didn't help the situation that grew in my pants every time I thought of her swinging her hips on the dance floor. My mate could dance. And fate had a seriously fucked-up sense of humor.

The phone rang as I contemplated rubbing one out again, giving me something else to focus on. I almost didn't answer it, knowing as soon as I saw the name on the screen that my day was about to go to shit. But apparently, being refused by your mate turned you into a masochist.

"What's up, Phoenix?" I asked when I swiped to accept the call.

"Hey man, I was just wondering if you had any time today to come out? I know you put in a lot of work with me yesterday, but I'd like to finish the downstairs today so I can start the nursery tomorrow, and I need a hand with the trim. Zuri's making ribs for lunch as payment."

I rubbed a hand over my face, wishing I were the kind of guy who could say no to a friend who needed me. But I couldn't... It wasn't in my nature.

Sighing, I glanced at the time. "No problem. I can be there in an hour."

"Thanks, Shadow. You're really helping me out."

"Anytime." I ended the call and tossed the phone on the bed. What the hell was I doing? Scarlett might be at Phoenix's place, and the last thing I needed was to spend more time trying not to notice every detail about her. But I couldn't leave the guy hanging, so I'd risk seeing the woman who hated me enough to defy fate if it meant helping him out. We were only days away from the charity ride to Chicago for Blaze's birthday celebration, and then I could blow out of town and not come back for a long time. Maybe ride with another den for a year or so as I swept up the remnants of my heart.

Lucky me.

Ten minutes later, I stood under the streaming water of my shower. The tile pressed cold against my hands, the water hot on my back, a nice juxtaposition of sensation to keep me grounded. Memories of Scarlett dancing flooded my mind whenever I closed my eyes, making me angry and hurt and horny all at once. Damn her for not giving us a try. She didn't even know me, had never said a word to me until she told me no. Yet she let that carbon copy Ken doll rub all up on her, she talked to him, she smiled at him. And my God, she was so beautiful when she smiled.

I took my heavy dick in my hand, unable to resist the need a moment longer. Fingers slick with soap, I squeezed almost to the point of pain before tugging, sliding, working myself toward completion. I set a quick pace; this wasn't a moment to draw out the pleasure. This was about getting mine and getting off for the sole purpose of relieving the pressure in my groin. Sliding my hand from base to tip and back, I tugged and squeezed, harder and faster, grunting when I purposely flicked the underside of the head on the way to the tip. Fuck yeah, that was good.

That hair, that skin, those damned green eyes all danced in my mind. But it was Scarlett's smile that had me groaning and pumping faster. The smile she gave someone else. The smile that had never been for me. The smile that made my heart almost put itself back together.

I came with a grunt, equal parts relieved, frustrated, and thoroughly pissed. The girl had already refused me; why couldn't I get her out of my mind? Why couldn't my soul let her go and head off to mourn the loss of our mate in peace?

Why couldn't I curl up and die in the forest the way my father had when my mother eventually rejected him?

TEN HOURS, ONE HUGE plate of ribs, and endless stories of what had been going on at the denhouse while I'd been out of town later, I was back at work with Phoenix finishing the toe kick along the baseboard we'd already installed. The whole first floor looked as if it belonged in a different house with the dark, hand-sawn flooring. More natural and warm. I liked it, and it fit the couple who lived there. A shifter and a witch in the middle of suburbia. That thought made me smirk.

As we moved to measure the last wall that needed trim, my heart nearly exploded in my chest. *Scarlett.* I felt her long before I heard her car, indicating our bond was growing stronger, not weakening, as I would have expected. She'd refused me; her not accepting the mating should have shattered my heart, not secured it to hers.

As she turned onto the gravel driveway, my stomach dropped and my hands shook, anxious dread making me sweat. My inner wolf surged forward, past all my nervousness, ready and willing to make an appearance. My tiger stalked, calm and ready to claim his mate. That burn, that fire she started within me when we met, roared to life. From a soft smolder to a raging inferno in a matter of seconds. And I'd thought my heart had already been incinerated. Silly me.

My ears picked up every motion, every swish and crinkle. The slide of her clothes against the leather seats, the slight crunch of her feet on the gravel, and the staccato beat of her heart as she stepped onto the porch. I waited, completely focused on the door even as my eyes looked over the ticks of the tape measure, my heartbeat matching hers. She waited as well, breathing hard, taking more seconds than normal before she walked inside without knocking. Before her scent and the need to be near her nearly knocked me off my feet.

"What's up, Scar?" Phoenix asked.

I didn't look up, didn't bother trying to see her. If she didn't want me, I'd make sure she didn't have to deal with me. I'd leave her alone to give her the chance to completely sever the bond between us, no matter how much it hurt. Once I finished installing this fucking moulding and got the hell away from this house, that is.

"Just came to drop some things off for Zuri." Her voice floated across the room, slicing through me, making me have to fight to hold back a whimper. "She around?"

"Kitchen." Phoenix turned on the saw, effectively covering all traces of Scarlett with the whine of the blade and the scent of sawdust.

"By the Goddess," Scarlett said with a rough laugh. "If she's barefoot, pregnant, *and* in the kitchen, I'm done."

Phoenix snorted. "You go and say that to her, Sparky. I'm

pretty sure she'll hailstorm your ass."

As they laughed and chatted, I knocked in a few more finishing nails before going back over them with the nail set to make sure the head sat below the surface of the wood. One more section, a little wood filler, and I could escape the hell that was being in the same space as the mate who didn't want me. Ten minutes, tops.

"You guys want a beer?" Zuri asked as she walked into the room. I looked up but kept my eyes on Phoenix's mate, ignoring the need to search out my own. Hardly even noticing the pretty turquoise sweater she wore or the way her multicolored hair tumbled in soft waves over her shoulders like liquid fire.

"Not me," I said, my voice a little hoarse. "But thank you for offering."

"We're almost done here, babe," Phoenix said. He held the next piece against the wall so I could nail it in place. Once secured, he moved behind me to set the nails so I could fill in the holes they left behind. Good man...eight minutes and counting.

"You going out with that same guy tonight?" Zuri asked. Time screeched to a halt, and my blood ran cold. Fuck and shit and all things wrong, no. Not now. I was barely holding on to my control. I didn't need to hear—

"Uh...yeah. He's coming to pick me up in a bit."

Some kind of nail and coffin analogy flitted through my memory, but I was too far gone to grasp it. My mate didn't want me; she wanted another. A man she allowed to breach those high walls of hers. To woo her. I closed my eyes for a moment and took a deep breath, fighting back the need to snarl. The tiger inside of me inched forward, still wary but ready to roar his displeasure as well. He wasn't the type to share. Hell, neither was I.

"Well, I appreciate you exchanging the sheets for me," Zuri said, oblivious to the war raging within me. "I haven't felt much like driving lately."

I shook off my rage and pounded in the last nail, fighting the whole time to control the beasts within. My hands shook as I worked the filler into the holes, my body battling my mind. I wanted to look at Scarlett, wanted to talk to her, see her, touch her. To scale those fucking walls and get close to her. Wanted to make her *see* me not just as Phoenix's friend, but as a potential suitor or mate.

Instead, I focused on the nail and the hammer, smacking them down, banging louder and harder than was needed. She didn't want me. If she hadn't made that clear before, her going on a date with someone else was enough to set that burn deep. She'd chosen someone else over me, probably the Ken doll from the bar. Someone who appeared to be the exact opposite of me, with his pressed pants and collared shirts, his perfectly-in-place blond hair and his all-American look. I was a jeans and T-shirt guy, a helmet-head or windblown kind of man, one with inky black hair like my mother's people and a slight tilt to my eyes that gave away the ancestors who came to America on a boat too many generations before me. If what she wanted was the guy from the bar, I had absolutely no shot. My chance was over before it had ever begun.

I just wished my animal sides would get that through their heads.

"Anytime. You know I'll help you however I can," Scarlett said, making my heart clench at the sound of her voice. Sweet... The kind of woman who took care of those she loved. I liked that about her, saw it as a positive trait. One I wouldn't see directed my way...ever.

The girls went silent as we worked, but I could feel Scarlett's interest. She flooded me with a sense of being watched, a little heat where there should be none.

"Shit, it's getting late," she said suddenly, as if she'd only just realized the time. "I should probably get back. Don't want

Doug waiting on the porch."

Her words slowed as she ended her sentence, her voice growing almost uncertain. Not that I was paying her all of my attention. Filling nail holes was far more vital to my sanity than figuring out why the girl may not be thrilled about going on her date. With another man. A man named Doug who wore pleated khakis to a bar and probably used more hair spray than Scarlett and her sisters combined.

Distracted from the job at hand, I slipped, spreading wood filler across the paint above the trim. Damn it.

"Be careful, Scar," Phoenix said, his eyes trained on the piece of wood in front of him. "Make sure Amber knows where you are and when to expect you home."

I caught myself just before I nodded in agreement. She may not have wanted to be mine, but that didn't mean I couldn't care about her safety. I appreciated Phoenix looking out for my… For her.

"Yeah, yeah, I know, brother dear. Constant vigilance and all that."

I kept my eyes on the tinted filler, totally ignoring the feel of her gaze on my back. Because I did feel it. A burning tickle, a pressure of sorts, searing me as I fought not to return it. She needed to leave. She needed to turn away and just go. She'd made her choice, and I could live with it if I didn't have to be around her. But instead she stared at me, waiting me out it seemed, watching me for some kind of reaction. One that I refused to give her.

"Are you leaving or did you suddenly take an interest in woodworking?" Zuri asked with a laugh. I closed my eyes as the pressure from Scarlett's gaze slipped away, loving and hating the sense of release.

"Sorry. Yeah, just…stuck in my head."

The softness of Scarlett's tone spoke to me, forced me to turn. To seek out her eyes. To surrender. She was looking back at me, staring, her expression not at all what I'd expected. She actually looked to be in some kind of emotional pain. Sad, almost. Perhaps feeling the same pull to me as I did to her.

"I should—" she paused, shook her head a little "—I need to go." Her eyes flicked away and back, meeting mine for a moment that seemed to last a lifetime. God, the tug to bond with her was more brutal when her eyes were locked with mine. The need to be next to her so intense, I had to grip my ankle with one hand to keep from jumping up and stalking in her direction. She needed to go, all right. She needed to stay away from me if she didn't want my attention. And I needed to go back to Chicago where I wouldn't see her anymore and could lick my wounds.

The thought of leaving, of running away like a coward, didn't sit well with me, but I was beginning to see it as my only option. For whatever reason, my soul refused to take the hint that she had no interest in me. Instead of fading or breaking, the draw to her only increased with every moment. I needed to escape. To get away before I acted on the need demanding I pull her into my arms and kiss the ever-loving hell out of her. She didn't want me, and I had to respect that.

Yet, as she walked out the door, she turned around to take a final look. Her eyes met mine again, bright and wide and filled with something almost like a longing. Which couldn't be... She'd refused me. She'd told me no. That should have been the end of it. Nowhere in the histories I'd read of both sides of my shifter heritage did it mention second chances for refused mates. It didn't happen. If the mate refused you, you walked away and either suffered through decades of emotional torment or you died. End of story.

So why was Scarlett looking at me as if she didn't want to walk away?

And why were my inner beasts still screaming out *mine*?

SIX

Scarlett

DAMN THAT SHADOW AND his ridiculously handsome face. The man was going to drive me to drink. All week, I'd had to replay visions of him in my head. The curve of his back as he turned away, the muscles bulging in his arm as he hammered on that piece of wood, the way his fingers pinched the nails from between his lips. But the worst, the absolute showstopper of my little Shadow-movie from Zuri's house, was the look he gave me when I was leaving. The way he seemed to look all the way inside of me practically set my soul on fire with those gray eyes of his.

That look had wrecked me.

But that was it…one look, and he went right back to work. Did he not feel the same turmoil I did when we were in the same room? Did he not notice the connection that seemed to grow stronger with every day? I rocked and searched for solid ground, adrift on a sea of the unknown, and he pounded in nails as if all this fated soul bond crap was nothing. As if I was nothing.

Well, screw that.

If he was going to make it a habit to be in my world,

I'd make it a habit to be in his. Starting with his Feral Breed denhouse. The wolf shifters were hosting some charity ride to Chicago to celebrate the birthday of their leader. Beast had asked me to help with the plans a month or so ago, but I hadn't wanted to deal with being at the denhouse because Amber had been hounding me about one of the dogs being my red thread.

And damn, I hated it when she was so very right.

Still, today wasn't about Amber, it was about Shadow. The man whose eyes practically sent me straight to ashes on the wind, especially when they passed right over me. Shadow, who barged into my life without my asking. He came onto my turf and upset my world, so I'd do the same to him. I'd infiltrate his private space and make sure he knew who the hell I was. No sense hiding from the shifters or the den any longer... My fear had been realized.

I followed Amber to the Feral Breed denhouse with my head high, my heels clacking, and my skirt a little too short for a casual afternoon of working out event details. Immature, maybe, but I wanted to make a damned point. I could catch a man's eye...maybe not my own red thread's, but someone in this denhouse would notice me. I'd make sure of it. Not to mention, Shadow looked like some kind of bad-boy-gone-good rock star in his dark T-shirts and the faded-to-perfection jeans that hugged his ass in a way that should have been illegal. I needed to up the ante on this game.

As soon as I walked in the door, every head turned my way. Daunting, and yet exactly what I wanted. Cocking my hip, refusing not to see this plan through even as all those not-quite-human eyes stared, I smiled and waved.

"Hello, boys."

There was a grumble of greeting from the various men in black leather. Not quite a resounding welcome, but something better than going wolf and taking a chunk out of my leg. Or pissing on it. Didn't dogs do that? Something about territory...

Whatever. No bite, no piss, I was happy.

Amber rolled her eyes and dragged me across the room, always the responsible one. I let her, not really wanting to be out here anyway. Still, I grinned and shrugged as we passed the bar, smiling at the men sitting and watching some kind of car race on the big screens. I might need their attention later if Shadow showed up.

"C'mon, Hester Prynne. Rebel's office is down here." Amber yanked me along a hallway, almost knocking me off my feet.

I pulled my arm from her hold. "You could ease up a bit."

"And you could act like an adult now and again."

I smirked. "Oh, I'm an adult all right. You can take my word on that one."

"Could have fooled me," she said, her voice soft but tight. I followed her to the back of the club, past men of all ages and sizes, making sure to put a little extra swing in my hips. Even before I looked, I knew the moment Shadow walked into the bar behind me. I sensed him, felt him in the tug of the thread around my heart. I nearly trembled at the pull, almost faltered in my stride at the weight of his eyes on my back. But I stayed strong, walking tall and working every curve I had.

That's right, buddy. I'm in your denhouse. Deal with it.

"Hey, ladies." Rebel stood when we turned into his office, a wide smile on his face.

Charlotte hurried around the desk to greet us with hugs. "Thank you so much for coming. I was getting a little overwhelmed with everything."

"It's no problem," Amber said. "We're glad to help."

"Great." She turned to give Rebel a good-natured glare. "You...go do your thing. I've got this covered."

Rebel laughed and pulled her close, kissing her nose and cheeks before pressing his lips to hers. The kiss looked soft and sweet, filled with so much emotion it almost hurt to watch. The thread around my heart drew tighter, making me ache. Making me burn for something I was missing. I wanted that kind of connection to someone, I really did. But I wanted to choose the other half of the equation, not let the Fates decide for me. I'd lived my life following someone else's rules, why couldn't I follow my own for once?

"Behave," Rebel whispered against Charlotte's lips before taking a step back. He walked out the door with a casual, "Have fun, ladies. Try not to talk about my four-hundred-year-old dick, Miss Scarlett."

I leaned out the door and grinned, remembering the first time I'd actually hung out with his mate. "I'll do my best."

Rebel shook his head, chuckling as he made his way to the bar. To the other guys in the club. To Shadow. I felt a need to follow him, to search out the end of my red thread, but I walked back into the office instead. I would not surrender.

"So," Charlotte said, looking excited and a little flustered. "We have around sixty people signed up so far to come to the kickoff party, though not all will be riding. That's the responsibility of hangers-on and the Pups of the club. The patched guys are handling the logistics of the ride to Chicago themselves. We're in charge of the charity carnival that will be held at the park where the ride will end."

Amber gave me a sidelong glance, probably checking to make sure I wasn't ready to run yet. "What do we need to do?"

Five hours and what felt like a hundred conversations later, I walked back into the bar area. My head hurt, my throat was raw, and I never wanted to make another phone call for the rest of my life. Amber and Charlotte were still at it, setting up rides and food booths and working out contract issues. My part was done for now, though, and I needed whiskey…stat.

"Can I get a little Jack?" I said to the guy behind the bar as I settled onto one of the high stools. Sadly, it wasn't him who answered.

"I can give you a big Jack."

I turned and glared at the jerk sitting two seats down, the one who apparently thought I was looking for more than a drink. "I wasn't talking to you."

"No, but I'm talking to you." He stood and moved to my side, his arm on the back of my seat. Almost caging me in against the bar. Sparks lit in my blood and my vision turned a very dangerous shade of orange. I was tired, cranky, and not in the mood for his kind of bullshit. This couldn't possibly end well.

The short fucker leaned closer, looking me up and down as if I were a piece of meat in the butcher's window. "Why don't you come with me to the back? I'm sure I've got what you need."

I rolled my eyes. "Honey, I have heels taller than you. Why don't you head back there without me? I'm sure you know exactly how to flog your own bishop."

Turning back to the bar, I tried to ignore the Napoleon wannabe, but his eyes kept traveling up and down my body, leaving behind a slimy, cold sensation that made me want to gag...or run. That particular instinct pissed me off even more, though. I wasn't weak. I could fight if I needed to. My coven had made me run from everything when I was with them, but no longer. I'd stand my ground, even when the ground wasn't technically mine to stand on.

A finger running up my leg sent my mind spinning into flames so hot, they burned my ears with their roar.

"You need to be a little nicer to me, sweetheart. I'm important around here."

The room became bathed in a deep red light as my temper flared hot and bright in my mind. The elemental power of fire poured through me, blazing a trail down my back, liquid fire in my veins. My fingertips burned, ready to release the flames of my fury. This man was about to see why you didn't touch a fire witch unless she wanted you to, and sometimes not even then.

Spinning slowly to face him, I let my fire witch go. Let her out…let my power fly freely. I knew my hair had to be glowing at the ends, my fingertips bright orange with the flames ready to burst through, but I didn't care. If I couldn't light myself up around a pack of men who changed into animals at will, where could I?

"You need to get your hand off me," I hissed, my voice hard.

"Oh, this hand?" He wrapped his stubby fingers around my upper thigh. "This hand ain't doing you no harm."

I reared back, setting my fingertips ablaze in preparation for nailing this idiot in the face. The pain spread quickly, the unbalanced elemental power consuming me instead of working with me as it did when I had full control of my magick. But hell, I welcomed the burn of lighting my hands on fire. The pain would be worth it to make my point to this little prick. I'd happily burn a man like him, the ones who thought they had a right to my body even when I'd refused them. I had no problem teaching this one a painful lesson. But before I could strike, before I could even lift my hands enough to scare the douche, someone moved between us.

"The lady said to remove your hand from her leg."

Shadow loomed large over the other guy, his face hard and his shoulders set. A mountain of a man staring down at the short one who was no longer touching me. A low growl rumbled from Shadow, a sound that shot up my spine and made me shiver in my seat. As much as I hated the thought of needing a protector, there really was something incredibly hot about a Prince Charming coming to your rescue. But fuck if I'd admit that out loud. Ever. Especially not to the prince who might have wanted to lock me away in his tower.

The short fucker crossed his arms. "I don't remember asking for your advice, Shadow."

"And I don't remember you being such a prick, but here

we are," Shadow said, advancing a step, pushing the little guy farther away from me.

Shadow's arm brushed my leg as he angled himself more solidly between the short guy and me. The contact made my entire body flush with desire, so much I nearly whimpered. Good Lord, he needed to get away from me before I exploded.

"Magnus," Rebel hollered from across the room, glaring at the short shifter. "Come with me, now."

Shadow watched as the short guy stormed off, his glare still firmly in place, his growl a solid, sustained rumble.

And then he looked at me, sending my soul up in flames.

"You okay?"

Oh for the sake of the Goddess, his voice. The hard look in his eyes. The scent of him as he leaned close. He was killing me with his Shadow-ness, and that just pissed me off even more.

"I don't remember asking for your help," I said, infusing my voice with anger even as it wobbled. "I could have handled that on my own."

He seemed to be unable to look away, his eyes roaming over me as if in some kind of inspection. Not like Magnus had done, not checking out my assets, more checking out the state of said assets. Making sure I was okay. Caring about me.

"Of that, I have no doubt." He leaned in, and I swear he sniffed me. "But just because a person can handle a situation on their own doesn't mean I'm not going to jump in. Guys like Magnus don't hear women. Your no is meaningless to him, but mine bears weight. It sucks, but it's the way his mind works."

"Yeah, well." I shook my head, the fight draining out of me, the need to wrap myself around him so damn hard to resist. "I didn't need you to fight my fight for me."

"I never thought you did." His eyes went dark when he saw my hands. Every fingertip screamed, the skin an angry red color, burned from the flames I'd been preparing to use in my defense. I curled them into fists, hiding the evidence no matter how much they hurt.

"You sure you're okay?" His eyes met mine again. Deep, beautiful, the eyes of someone kind and caring. I wanted to get lost in them, to stare at him for hours. To press myself against him and—

"It's fine," I said as I shook off the pull of the red thread. Not real, I chanted in my head, trying to keep from acting on the wants the Fates showered me in when Shadow was around. "This is nothing. It happens all the time."

He frowned. "Looks painful."

"Only the first thousand times."

His eyes met mine again, and he raised a single eyebrow. Damn that look. It made him appear so smartass and sarcastic. And hot...definitely hot. Motherfucker.

"If you say so." He gave me one last look-over before turning and walking away, disappearing into the back hallways of the denhouse. Leaving me shaking at the bar. Alone again and no closer to understanding why I couldn't turn off the mating bond within me. Because I wanted to break that connection to him, and soon.

At least that's what I told myself.

SEVEN

Shadow

TWO HOURS AFTER THE incident with Magnus, and I still couldn't control my growling. All three sides of my personality were on the same side for once, and that agreement was wrapped around a sense of frustrating rage. The jackass had dared to touch my mate without her permission. He'd made her burn herself—set her own damn fingers on fire—to ward off his advances. Those red fingers, the obviously painful burns, had destroyed what control I'd found while being in the same building as her. I'd wanted to grab her and hide her away, wanted to protect her with my body. But that would have been a bad decision, as she hadn't seemed interested in having me help her in any way possible. That woman had some thick fucking walls around her, ones with turrets on top and guards with guns ready to shoot anyone who dared come near.

I'd had to leave the denhouse once I'd made sure Scarlett was okay. If I'd seen Magnus again—if I hadn't felt Rebel punished him enough—I probably would have challenged him to a true shifter brawl, one settled with claws and teeth and blood. And I would have won, even if I had to kill him. Even if I had to reveal my roar instead of my howl. But with the trouble brewing around the Omegas and my responsibilities in Chicago, I couldn't deal with the added drama of a dumbass shifter pushing me to out myself as a mixed breed.

Besides, Scarlett had made it abundantly clear…she didn't need or want my help.

Pacing, I ran a hand through my hair and sighed, growing more agitated by the moment. I was hungry…starving… famished. The call to shift to my wolf and run through one of the Metroparks south of the city was strong. The thought of having to deal with cooking or ordering or even lifting a fork to my lips did not appeal. My beasts wanted to hunt live prey, and I was almost ready to give in to that desire.

A sudden knock on the door made me spin and snarl, ready to attack. Rarely did I allow myself to fall so deeply into my thoughts that people could sneak up on me. This drama with Scarlett was truly messing with me.

Assuming one of my den brothers was on the other side of the door, I inched down the hall and sniffed, the shifter way of saying "Who's there?"

And then I whimpered.

Fire and ice, a light sooty flavor wrapped around lavender and snow creating a cocktail of seduction I'd know anywhere.

I rushed to the door. Scarlett had never come to my apartment before. Hell, she had only just come to the denhouse for the first time today. If she sought me out, there had to be something wrong. I would rip myself apart if Magnus pulled something again. If he'd hurt or scared her. Well, I'd rip myself apart after I destroyed him.

The door flew back as I yanked, leaving me standing in the opening and staring at my mate. Amazed. Scarlett stood in the hallway, sexy and adorable and *there* with some sort of covered dish in her hands. Her eyes locked with mine and she flushed, looking all kinds of uncomfortable and almost shy. Such an odd expression for her beautiful face. Brash and ballsy, tough…

that was Scarlett, not this shy little creature. She seemed more like Little Red Riding Hood coming to see the big bad wolf than a rough-and-tumble warrior with defenses made of stone.

But hell, as long as she was at my door, I was happy. She'd searched me out and brought me dinner, it seemed. Between the food and the scent of my mate so close, I practically drooled on the carpet.

"Zuri sent me. This. She sent this." She thrust the dish forward, trying and failing not to look at me. But look she did. I felt the burn of her gaze as it dropped down my body, responding with a quiet growl, liking the attention. She stared hungrily, her eyes absorbing me, consuming me. True, I had taken my shirt off when I came home, but I'd donned my old gray sweat pants as well. Baggy, ratty, and faded, they were something I never left the house wearing. I needed a shower, a shirt, and a pair of jeans to be presentable, yet my mate couldn't stop looking. Or rather, trying not to look.

With a sigh and a small shake of her head, she finally met my gaze. Her eyes stayed on mine as she placed the dish in my hands, being careful not to actually touch me.

"We've never really been introduced. I'm Scarlett Weaver, Zuri's sister, and this is for you."

"What is it?" I asked, not sure if I was asking about the dish or something else. Something more about her. About why she'd felt the need to come here when she could have sent Phoenix or Amber.

"Picadillo. It's a kind of stew." She tugged at the hem of her shirt, her eyes repeatedly darting to my chest as we stood mere inches away from one another. "It's a family thing, kind of. Our mother taught Aunt Sarah to make it before she died. My mom, not my aunt, that is. Before my mother died. Though they're both dead now. Not that it matters." Her eyes went wide as I cocked my head. "Oh God, not that it matters to you. It totally matters to me and my sisters. But you...probably not so much."

I pulled up one side of my mouth in a smile, fighting back my laughter as she blanched and scrunched up her nose.

"Damn it," she hissed before taking a deep breath and giving me a very strong stare. "It's a sort of Cuban stew, and it's delicious. Zuri makes it better than any I've ever had. You just have to heat it up."

I looked down at the dish, completely in shock that she'd bring me food. That she was, in some small way, taking care of me. It was such a mate thing to do. "Why?"

When my eyes met hers, I almost rocked back on my heels. So much emotion laced through the green. Confusion, reluctance, something that looked a lot like fear. I wanted to protect her, to help her, but I didn't know how. I didn't know what I could do other than leave her alone, but with her standing at my door offering me food, that option took a major dive into the backseat. The cracks in her walls were showing, and I wanted to explore every one of them.

Scarlett shrugged, focusing on the doorjamb instead of me. "Because you've been helpful. Phoenix and Zuri couldn't have laid all that flooring on their own, and it makes my sister happy to have one more thing ready for when the baby comes." Her voice dropped almost to a whisper and she finally graced me with her eyes again. "It's our way of saying thank you."

I nodded, not knowing what to say. No one had ever brought me food like this. And though there was no need for Phoenix and Zuri to thank me, their kindness brought Scarlett to my door. Something I hadn't thought would ever happen.

"How?" I lifted the dish a little and raised an eyebrow.

She smirked a bit, obviously regaining some of her confidence. "How, what…to eat it? With a spoon…or maybe a fork. And definitely with some bread. I brought a loaf from the bakery for you."

I grinned. "Thank you, but that wasn't what I meant. How

do I heat it up?"

"Oh, you're one of those guys who can't cook. Of course." Scarlett rolled her eyes and took the dish from my hands. "Are you hungry?"

"Always."

She walked past me, looking as if she belonged in my apartment, swaying her hips through my entryway and into the living room. I watched her go, practically hunting her with just my eyes. Jesus, she was in my den...my space...her scent mingling with mine. If she knew what that meant to the beasts within me, she'd probably run. My wolf howled in my mind with the excitement of getting our mate alone in our space. My tiger growled and stalked forward, ready to claim.

Scarlett looked back over her shoulder, almost catching me as I watched her walk away. She had a great ass; I couldn't be the only man who'd been unable to keep his eyes off it.

"I'll take care of this. Zuri would be pissed if you didn't like it because it was cold or you burned it. She went to a lot of trouble."

"I'll make sure to thank her," I said, closing the door. Scarlett hurried to my kitchen, which set off a ton of very inappropriate thoughts. Like her naked on my counters, ready for me to feast on her. The cabinets were the perfect height for me to kneel and—

"You like it hot?"

I jumped, my hand automatically moving in front of my groin, my palm brushing my hard cock and making me bite back a moan. Fucking sweat pants offered little in the way of support.

"Pardon?"

"Hot, as in spicy." She cocked her head as if knowing where my mind had been. "Do you like your food spicy or not?"

"Yeah," I replied, my voice rougher than normal, my eyes locked on hers so I didn't stare at her...other parts. "Spice is good. I like heat."

With a smirk and a shake of her head, she turned and started messing with the controls of the stove. She moved about my kitchen as if she knew it, like she'd been there a million times before. I sat at the little bar counter and bit back a cheesy grin, enjoying the view and the daydreams she inspired.

"So," she said as she placed the dish in the oven. "Shadow. Where'd that come from?"

I grinned. "Your sister asked me that same question the other day."

Scarlett lifted a shoulder in a lazy shrug. "We can't find the perfect curse if we don't know anything about you."

My face fell, and I sat back on my stool, that instinctual fear of witches flaring bright. But then Scarlett grinned.

"Kidding, wolf man. I'm just nosy."

I snorted a laugh, relaxing once more. "You're preying on my instincts."

"What instincts?" She looked at me with a question on her face, as if she honestly didn't know about the tension between our species.

"Shifters fear witches. It's practically tattooed on our minds at birth."

"So you're afraid of me?" She looked up at me, her lashes long, her green eyes piercing my soul.

"Terrified." My answer was honest but not entirely in line with what she'd asked. Not really. Her witch side made me nervous at times, but the bond I felt for her was what scared me. Was what had the power to crush me.

"Witches aren't big fans of shifters either, you know."

I nodded. "I assume because of the Hounds of God, though we're—"

"Not werewolves, I know." Scarlett leaned against the far counter, the curve of her hip attracting my attention for a brief moment. "Phoenix and Rebel were pretty clear about the distinction when we first met them. You shift at will, the witch-hunting werewolves are controlled by the moon."

"Exactly.

"Good to know." Her smile was small but bright, even a little sarcastic. "So back to this nickname—"

"Road name."

"Whatever." She rolled her eyes, but the smile tempered her sarcasm. "Why Shadow? Why not Rex or Fluffy?"

"I'm not a dog." I rolled my eyes back at her, making her chuckle. "I'm fast and quiet. People don't notice me until it's too late, and I'm sneaky. Gates said at my naming ceremony that my enemies wouldn't know I was there until the shadow of death fell upon them."

"Huh," she said, biting her lip and watching me. "I guess I can see that. So is that what you do? You…kill people?"

I swallowed hard, watching her, feeling her tension from across the room. Fuck me, how was I supposed to explain this?

Scarlett jumped and turned to check the oven, shaking her head. "Never mind, I didn't mean to—"

"No," I interrupted, leaning over the counter, afraid she'd run. "It's okay. I just…can't talk about a lot of it."

"Secret-agent-shifter stuff?"

"Sort of." I sat back and ran a hand through my hair, pulling it back. "Technically, I'm a doctor, so I'm usually involved in things that could go wrong so I'll be there to patch up any of the guys who need it. But lately, I've been working on another type of mission for the president of our group."

"What kind of mission?"

"One I can't talk about. One that makes me use my sneaky side more than my doctor one…for the most part."

"Oh," she said, looking wary and slightly defensive. "So you…sneak around?"

I shrugged. "I spy a bit when need be."

"And what would make there be a need to spy? What…

some rival shifter gang edging in on your turf?"

I shook my head. "No, nothing that simple. I spy because there are lives at stake, innocent lives. And many of them. I do this to keep good people safe and to find out all I can about the bad ones."

"Huh." She checked the oven again, turning her back to me but not before I saw the way the tension left her face, how her shoulders relaxed. "I guess that's okay."

We didn't chat much more as the dish heated, only bits of small talk. Weather, the upcoming ride, weather, den members who'd made an impression on her, more weather. Boring stuff, normally, but I wouldn't have traded a single second of that time. I spent half an hour with my mate in my kitchen talking about *the weather*, and it was perfect.

"How're your fingers?" I asked when she finally pulled the dish out of the oven, her hands tucked inside the black oven mitts I'd never used. She pulled the gloves off, the slight coloring of the tips of her fingers catching my attention and making me itch to examine them.

"Fine." She shrugged and grabbed a wooden spoon, dishing the stew into a bowl she'd grabbed out of my cupboard. "I'm an elemental witch with an affinity for fire. Seriously, my temper's been setting my fingers on fire since I was a teenager. It's no big deal."

She laid a full bowl in front of me that smelled like the food version of heaven. Warm and spicy, with just a little sweetness, it reminded me very much of her. But when she tried to back away, the food became a secondary concern. Without thought, I grabbed her hand, frowning at the scars and the new burns still visible in the reddened skin of her fingers.

"It's a big deal if it hurts." I traced along the edge of a scar, the mottled skin smoother than I thought it'd be. Perhaps a quick healing response ran through witches like it did through shifters. My fingers traced the marks, examining the texture and the heat below it. Her skin burned to the touch, not just the damaged portions, but all of it. As if there was a fire inside of her. As if her affinity for fire was more than that, was something deep in her blood. In her makeup. She didn't just like fire or favor it, she *was* fire.

Scarlett's hands shook and her breathing sped up as my fingers stroked hers. I wondered if anyone had ever touched her like this—gently, and with concern for something that was simply a part of her nature.

As my finger ran over the base of her nail, she snatched her hands back. "Everything hurts eventually."

"Not everything. I don't believe that."

"That's been my experience." Scarlett took a deep breath and handed me a spoon. "Try it."

I glanced at her fingers, my brow pulling down. "What?"

"The picadillo." She caught my eyes, smiling stiffly, imploring me to move on from what was obviously a personal subject. "Quit worrying about things neither of us can control and try the food, Shadow."

I took the utensil she offered, goose bumps erupting on my arm when our fingers brushed. They appeared on her arm as well, both of us obviously affected by the casual touch of the other. Interesting, and altogether confusing. I was still staring at her arms and thinking over what all this could possibly mean when the first spoonful of stew hit my tongue.

"Holy shit." I stared up at her, wide-eyed.

"If Zuri hears you call her food shit, she'll kill you."

I shook my head and loaded up a second spoonful. "This is...amazing."

She shrugged a single shoulder. "Yeah, it kind of is."

"No kind of about it." I dug in, enjoying the way the heat and the spice balanced so nicely with the underlying sweetness. The flavors warmed me more with every bite, making me wish my meal would never end. Though the company could have had a hand in that want as well.

Scarlett stood on the other side of the counter, watching me, smiling.

"Have some." I nodded toward the kitchen.

She shook her head even as her eyes darted to my bowl. "I'll get some next time Zuri makes it."

I rolled my eyes and grabbed her hand, dragging her around to my side of the bar. "Have some pickle-dilla with me, Scarlett."

"Pic-a-dill-o," she said, stressing each syllable.

"Picadillo," I whispered in response, mimicking her pronunciation. Scarlett stared at my mouth, all flushed and hungry. Needy. Attracted. Walls crumbling.

Giving in to my need to take care of her, I picked up a piece of the bread she'd sliced earlier and dipped a chunk in the sauce before holding it up. Offering it to her. Feeding her.

"Open wide."

She glanced at the bread. "Well, now you sound like a doctor."

"Because I am one. Now open."

She parted those kissable pink lips slowly, obviously fighting her own reservations about trusting me. I placed the bite of food carefully on her tongue, keeping my eyes on hers and fighting back a growl.

She smiled and nodded as she swallowed. "It's good."

I stared, completely focused on a single drop of sauce clinging to her mouth. I wanted to lick it off. Craved the taste of her on my tongue. But instead, I ran my thumb over her bottom lip, capturing the drop.

"It's perfect." Holding her gaze, I brought my thumb to my mouth and licked off the bit of picadillo there, nearly moaning at the way her green eyes practically glittered with heat.

She bit her lip and dropped her gaze to my mouth before giving me a slow shake of her head. "Nothing's perfect."

"Why so negative, Scarlett Weaver?" I asked. I held up another piece of the bread dipped in picadillo, smiling when she immediately opened her mouth for me. Trusting me more than the first time. But my smile fell when her lips practically wrapped around the bread, millimeters from my fingers. Such a sexy visual. I was going to be hard for a week.

When she swallowed her bite, she shook her head. "I'm not negative, and you never told me your name."

I gave her a raised eyebrow again. "You know it's Shadow, and you're definitely negative."

After accepting and swallowing another bite, she rolled her eyes. "I'm a realist, that's all."

"You're scared." I offered her another bite, one she didn't take. Instead, she stared at me, her gaze intense and deep.

"Maybe, but I'm not weak."

"I never thought for a second that you were." I lifted the bread to her mouth again. This time, she allowed me to place the bite in her mouth, closing her lips around my fingers before I could pull away. The growl I released came out of nowhere, a deep and animalistic sound that made her shiver.

I yanked my hand back. "Sorry."

"For what?"

"Growling. I…didn't mean to."

She shrugged, taking my spoon from my hand. "It's okay. It's who you are."

"Part of," I whispered, watching her. Waiting for her to run. "It's only part of who I am."

She froze, watching me for a long moment before collecting a spoonful of picadillo. She lifted the utensil to my mouth but held it just out of my reach.

"What's your real name, Shadow of the Feral Breed?"

I opened my mouth for the bite, but she held the spoon away. Waiting. Wanting answers before she'd give up the stew. Before she'd give in.

"Zeev," I whispered, the name not something I'd heard or said since I'd become a pup within the Feral Breed several years before. "My name is Zeev Rimau."

"Zeev Rimau, a guy who growls, sneaks up on people, and likes picadillo." She smiled, eyes soft as they held mine. "I think I'll stick with calling you Shadow, though. It fits you. Now open."

Her voice was little more than a whisper, but it screamed in the tense air between us. Called to me. I opened as directed, reaching up to hold her wrist in place as she guided the spoon into my mouth. The food barely registered, only green eyes on mine and soft skin under my fingers. Skin I wanted to feel more of. A warmth grew within me, one brought on by the feel of her accepting my touch, radiating down my arm and outward through the rest of my body.

"If I'm the guy who growls," I murmured, not wanting to scare her off. "Who are you?"

She shrugged, her expression falling. "I'm the girl who sets shit on fire."

Her face stayed flat, serious, but there was something in her eyes that reached out to me. A little sadness, a tinge of insecurity. This firecracker had a vulnerable side, and it surprised me that I would get to see it so soon. Those walls didn't just have cracks, they had big, gaping holes.

I wrapped her hand in mine, gently tugging her closer "There's more to you than that. I can sense it."

And just like that, she shuttered herself off. Shoulders stiff, eyes dull and lifeless, lips pulled into a flat line. "Of course there is, but that's all you get for tonight." She pulled her hand from my grasp, dragging her fingers over my palm. Giving me one final tease before pushing me away.

"I think it's time for me to say goodnight." She brushed past me, closed off once more. But I'd seen that softer side, sensed her attraction to me. I knew there was something holding her back, but not enough to actually break the mating bond. She wanted me, and that scared her. But I could work with fear. Disgust, no. Hate, no. Fear, absolutely.

"What about tomorrow?" I asked as she made her way to the door.

"What about it?"

"Do I get more tomorrow?"

She huffed, acting irritated, but I couldn't miss the flush of her cheeks or the smile tugging at her lips. "We'll see."

EIGHT

Scarlett

SHADOW WAS SCOWLING AT his phone again. Not that I cared, or noticed, or was staring. Damn him for hanging out in the denhouse, being all handsome and scruffy and broody. I'd been working all morning and into the afternoon to organize the fair following the charity ride, and at first it'd been almost peaceful. But then Shadow showed up, and he said nothing to me. No hello, no good morning. He'd been sitting in the corner with a notepad and his phone the whole time, completely ignorant of the fact that I was in the same room. Even as the pull toward him nearly strangled me.

I really needed to snip this red thread before it tied me in knots.

Charlotte sat at the bar with a very sexy-looking Rebel, the two of them being all flirty and adorable. She'd brought her brother with her this time. Julian was a nice kid if a bit awkward and gangly. Those teenage years could be hellish. Still, he'd said thank you when I brought him a pop, which earned a bit of a nod from me. Good manners were hard to find sometimes. My eyes flicked to Shadow at that thought. He was a man with manners. Polite and charming, with a ridiculous chest and hard abs and a full Adonis belt cut on each his hipbones. A damned testament to the metabolism of shifter men.

Also, who would have known how hot sweat pants could be? The fact that the man could make those nasty old things he'd been wearing last night look so good just irritated me. No one should be that sexy wearing heavy-knit cotton.

Unable to resist, I snuck another peek across the room. Shadow sat in the same spot, still frowning, still staring at his phone, still handsome enough to make my heart stutter a bit. Still not noticing me in the slightest. Damn him.

Sighing, I stood and headed toward Rebel's office where Julian was supposed to be hanging out in front of the television. I needed to make a few phone calls, and that was where all the carnival documents were stored. Plus I couldn't stand to be ignored by Shadow a moment longer. It was seriously messing with my head, especially after the way he'd acted last night. How had we gone from flirty talk to not even a hello in so few hours? What was his deal?

Just before I reached the office, the door to the rear parking lot flew open and two of the largest men I'd even seen came storming inside. The hair on the back of my neck stood up as they stalked toward me, both scowling. I sensed the energy around them, saw the aura of violence and rage they projected. These two were not to be fucked with, but there was a teenager on the other side of the door to my side—a blind one. I couldn't let them get near Julian.

"You lost?" I asked, crowding close to the door and mentally calling to the corners. Keeping my magick close to the surface would be prudent considering the two towered over me. My skin tightened, a slow, hot sensation that spread from my fingers up my arms as my magick built within. The ache grew, every inch of me reacting to the burn of the flames licking through my veins. To the power flowing through me.

The shorter of the two growled loud and deep, barely even

bothering to flick his eyes in my direction. "Shadow. Now."

I threw out both arms as they moved to walk past me, to the door behind which Julian probably sat. The burn inside of me intensified, causing me to shiver as flames sparked at my fingertips.

"He's not in here."

Bigger finally looked down at me, his eyes practically glowing, sending a wave of power through my blood as my magick side sensed danger. *Shit shit shit.*

"Get the fuck out of the way, witch. We have business with Shadow."

I leaned toward them, refusing to give up my post in front of the office door but not willing to send them storming into the bar area either. If I could protect Julian, I could protect Shadow. In theory. "And there's a human boy in there who doesn't need to know whatever your business is, so I suggest you call Shadow on the phone and let him come to you."

The bigger man growled, creeping closer, crowding me against the door as he snarled. "I said, get out of the way."

A wave of power washed over me, cooling my fire for a single moment. A force not my own. My rage intensified, the burn coming back hotter and stronger, each hand engulfed in blue flames. Whatever magick he was trying to pull off wasn't going to work on me. No way, no how.

"And I told you no." I glared back at the beast of a man, burning inside and out as my protective instincts surged. Screw them, no one was getting past me. Julian was just a kid and, to be honest, as strong as Shadow seemed to be, these two dark-haired giants looked as if they could mop the floor with him. Literally. But they'd have to get through me before they even tried. I protected my own, and Shadow was kind of mine.

"Fuck this." As Smaller went to push past me, I silently chanted to my element and urged the flames centered on my hands to burn brighter, making sparks shoot from my fingers.

Grabbing Smaller's arm, I directed my flames to my palms. Searing him and burning myself in the process.

Smaller roared in pain, pulling back, yanking me almost off my feet. The smell of singed hair and flesh made me nauseous, but I couldn't let go. I couldn't let him get past me. I couldn't let him get to Julian.

Or Shadow.

Smaller roared again and swung at me. Bigger edged around the side of me, trying to knock me back. Grasping, releasing my own pain in a low growl worthy of any of these animals, I clung to Smaller's arm as hard as I could. The two men pulled and pushed, trying to get their hands on me, trying to win, but my heat kept them back. The burn of my protective element too much to come close to for long. I rode out their attacks, shaking and concentrating on increasing the fire through the pain radiating through my chest and up my arms. Blisters formed—his skin, mine, I couldn't tell. Couldn't see past the brightness of the first to recognize arms and hands. But I held on. I fought. I protected. And I set the three of us on fire.

When Smaller snarled and lunged at me as if to bite, I kicked out, striking his thigh and forcing him to one knee. Before I could adjust to the new position, Bigger grabbed me from the side, wrapping his arms around me and squeezing to the point that my ribs popped. I kicked and twisted, my arms burning bright all the way to my shoulders, but to no avail. He had me completely locked in his hold with my feet dangling, unable to move or even breathe. Through the flames and the burns and the heat, he held on. Crushing me.

But then a growl sounded from behind us, one I recognized. One that made my heart drop and flutter at the same time as my flames disappeared back under my skin.

With no other warning, something hard and heavy hit Bigger from behind, knocking us both to the ground. My attacker landed on top of me, his weight crushing me into the concrete. Shadow stormed over, grabbing Bigger by the shoulder and literally tossing him into the wall with one arm. As the concrete cracked under the force of Bigger's body slamming into it, Shadow grabbed me by the elbow and dragged me to my feet, gentle but demanding. I whimpered when his hand touched my burnt flesh, but otherwise let him manhandle me.

"Did they hurt you?"

I shook my head, leaning into his hold, letting my body relax against his as my adrenaline pumped. "Pretty sure I did the hurting myself."

Shadow snarled, holding me tight and angling his body to stand between me and the other men. "You touch her again, and I'll have your pelts. I don't care who you think you know."

"The bitch attacked me," Smaller cried, holding his blistered arms against his chest.

Shadow took a step forward, but I grabbed his belt loops and held tight, pulling my chest flush with his back. I clutched at him, desperate for the feel of his skin against mine, shaky and cold in the aftermath of the fight. His muscles relaxed even as his growl grew harsh and loud. One hand slid around to hold on to my hip, to pull me tighter, to hold me close to him. And I didn't mind a single bit. The fear and the pain and the sudden loss of adrenaline left me cold and tired. I didn't want even an inch between us.

Bigger smirked, looking from Shadow to me and back. Noticing my hands on Shadow's waist and his on my hip. Calculating. "You want a filthy witch, have her, but know that Blasius will be hearing about this."

He pushed Smaller down the hall, heading for the bar area of the building. "If she ever burns me or a packmate of mine again, her head will be mounted on my wall."

"Didn't anyone ever teach you about fire?" Shadow asked, turning us both to watch the men walk away. "If you get too close to the heat, you're going to get burned. Stay away from her, and you'll be fine."

Smaller scowled and spat before growling a simple, quiet, "Mutt."

Shadow lunged, striking Smaller in the jaw and drawing blood before the man could even spin all the way around. The two fell to the floor, swinging and growling as the sounds of fists meeting flesh echoed down the hall. Bigger rushed past me along with another dark-haired man, this one even bigger than Bigger. Biggest? They worked together trying to pull the two men off one another. I wanted to jump in, to protect Shadow, but my adrenaline crash was in full swing, and I could barely take a step without stumbling.

"What the fuck is going on back here?" Rebel rushed around the corner, looking angrier than I'd ever seen him. He shoved past the larger men and grabbed Shadow, stepping between him and Bigger. Relief flooded me as Rebel protected my Shadow, making my body sag. I backed into the wall and slid down to the floor, unable to stay on my feet a moment longer.

My Shadow…oh hell.

"Do you know there's a witch here?" Smaller asked, glaring at Shadow but yelling at Rebel.

"Yeah, I do." Rebel shrugged and crossed his arms over his chest, daring the other shifter to say more.

Bigger stepped beside his smaller counterpart, his hands up as if in retreat. "Can we quit wasting time? We need to talk to Shadow."

Shadow backed toward me, keeping himself between me and the strangers. "Head into Reb's office. I'll be there in a minute."

Biggest stepped toward him. "We don't have time for your—"

"I said Reb's office." Shadow stepped right up to the three, appearing unafraid by the men who towered over him. "Cahill should probably head to the bar so Klutch can take care of those burns. You two, office. If you want my help, you play by my rules. Otherwise you can keep on driving to Chicago."

"Julian's in there," I whispered, rising to my feet with one hand solidly against the wall. I once again pressed myself against Shadow's back, clinging to his strength and warmth. "That's why I was trying to stop them."

The three men looked past Shadow, Smaller sending me a glare that probably should have made my knees shake. Rebel's growl made him pull up quick, though.

"There's a human child in that room, and you choose to get into a fight with the fire witch who's trying to protect him?"

Bigger frowned. "We were looking for Shadow."

"Yeah, well, by the blood on his knuckles, I can see you found him." Rebel hurried into his office, almost immediately reappearing with a curious-looking Julian. "Deal with your shit, but if you threaten or start a fight with any of my den again, including our non-member guests, your asses are mine. C'mon, Cahill. You can spend a little time with my road captain. Shadow? Want to take a look at his burns?"

"Nope," Shadow said, staring at the remaining two strangers. "Let Klutch handle him. She needs me more."

Rebel looked over Shadow, an inquisitive expression on his face as his eyes traveled to where I had my arms wrapped around the shifter. "You sure?"

Shadow growled low and deep. "Yeah, positive."

I slipped back, releasing my hold on Shadow, uncomfortable with the attention the other shifters in the hall were giving us. Rebel met my gaze and cocked his head, inspecting. Making me shrink back. But then he shook his head.

"I don't think I want to know. Wait here, I'll be right back." Rebel turned and walked down the hall, bringing Julian and Smaller, or Cahill, with him. Bigger and Biggest walked into Rebel's office without another word and slammed the door behind them, leaving Shadow and me alone in the hallway.

"Are you okay?" Shadow asked, turning to look me over.

"I'm fine." I wrapped my arms around myself, being careful with my burns. "Who are they?"

He shrugged and shook his head. "A group of shifters from down south."

"They seem like assholes, especially the smaller one. Cahill." I smiled as Shadow snorted a laugh. "They refused to listen to me when I told them they needed to call you before they went storming into Rebel's office. I didn't want them scaring Julian."

The look he gave me was filled with more meaning than I could comprehend, with a depth to his eyes that gutted me. "I'd be just as much of an asshole and just as pissed if the situation were reversed."

"What situation?"

He shook his head. "Nothing…never mind."

I brought my hand to his arm. "Secret-agent-shifter stuff?"

He nodded and stared down at me, breathing hard, so close I could feel the heat rolling off his body in waves. I wanted him closer, wanted to feel more of him. Wanted to wrap myself around him and hold on tight.

Beyond the tug of my thread and the call of the Fates, I wanted him. And that might have been the scariest thing to think about all day.

"Soot." Shadow swallowed hard, running a finger down the side of my face. "You burned yourself."

"Happens all the time," I whispered, mesmerized by him.

His eyes danced along my face, my jaw, my neck. "You're okay, though, right? They didn't hurt you?"

"No."

"Liar." With soft hands, he untangled my arms, gently stroking above the burn marks. "You need a salve for these burns."

I shrugged, my heart racing and my mouth dry. "Not really. I'm used to it."

"I hate that you do this to yourself." He looked up at me again, inching closer, pressing himself against me as he lowered his voice and whispered, "They scared you."

It wasn't a question, more a statement of fact. And though normally I would have brushed it off with sarcasm, I could only nod.

"I'm sorry I wasn't paying more attention."

I shook my head. "It's not your fault."

He looked pained, at war with himself, before he let me go and took a step back. "I shouldn't have been so distracted. I promise to do better, to pay more attention to you."

I raised my eyebrows and wrapped my arms around myself, cold again now that he'd left me behind. "What if I say no?"

Shadow smiled, soft and sweet and meaning more to me than he could have ever known. He leaned over me, bringing his face so close, I could feel his breath on my cheek, the warmth of his skin. And then he growled.

"Whether you need me or not, I'll never let anyone hurt you."

NINE

Shadow

"WHAT THE HELL DID you think you were doing out there?" I stormed through the open door, ready to smash some mountain-shifter heads. Rebel smirked as he slid in behind me, plopping into his chair and kicking his feet up on his desk, the picture of cocky ease.

"What the hell do you think you're doing with an out-of-control fire witch?" the larger of the two asked.

"The witches are with us," Rebel replied, a growl to his voice. "They're guests of the Feral Breed and accepted by our team, which includes President Blasius Zenne. That girl or any of the others you may meet here are not to be touched."

The visiting shifter glared but nodded, understanding an Alpha's rule when he heard one. As he should… Killian O'Shea was Alpha to his own pack located deep in the Appalachian Mountains. They were new to the NALB and had unfortunately been both highly blessed and sorely injured over the past few months. Blessed that the pack had attended their first Gathering in December, the yearly social event where packs of the NALB came together to meet and hopefully find their fated mates. The Southern Appalachia pack had gone home with six new mates, including a shewolf named Lyra, who was Killian's other half. They also brought a shewolf named Kalie home with them. Mated to Gideon Kelly, the smaller visiting shifter in the room, Kalie was an Omega. And like all Omegas, she had been honored by the mountain pack... She'd been positively cherished, especially by Gideon.

Until she became another victim of the Omega kidnappers.

A group of shifters had infiltrated the pack and stolen Kalie away in February, killing many of their packmates and nearly killing Gideon himself in the battle. Killian and Gideon along with Killian's sister Moira, one of the two mates of Blaze, had been obsessively searching for the missing Omega, trying to use Gideon's mating bond to find her. But the kidnappers had figured out a way around the bond, leaving Gideon nothing but static where her pull should have been and frustrating all of us searching for her.

"So what's the situation?" Rebel asked, glancing from one to the other. "Someone want to fill me in?"

I stared at Killian. He hadn't wanted word of how the kidnappers had almost decimated his pack to get out, but I'd told him we might need to tell a few of the guys if we were going to get my den's help to find Kalie. Still, I left the decision up to him. His pack, his secret, his choice.

"This is Killian," I said, nodding toward the two visiting shifters, "Alpha of the Southern Appalachia pack, and his packmate, Gideon. The guy Scarlett lit up is Cahill. Guys, this is Rebel, president of the Great Lakes Feral Breed den. A man I trust and respect."

Killian sighed and gave me a scowl before angling himself toward Rebel. "Shadow's been working with us to find our kidnapped Omega packmate who's mated to Gideon here. Their bond since those bastards took her has been staticky at best and damn near nonexistent at worst. Until yesterday."

"What happened yesterday?" Rebel asked.

"I felt Kalie." Gideon leaned forward, a fanatical gleam in his eyes. "One minute there was nothing, and the next, I was up and moving and ready to race through the woods to get to her."

"They called Jameson," I said, meeting my den president's surprised eyes. "He and I have been partnered up for the past few months on this case."

Gideon nodded. "Killian, Cahill, and I jumped in the truck and headed in the direction of the pull right away. We also called Jameson as Blaze had instructed us to do. We were on our way through Ohio when the bond went quiet again, but not as quiet. I can feel her, but it's as if there's a veil between us."

Rebel groaned and leaned back, his eyes hard and filled with anger. "Are they drugging her?"

I shrugged. "Jameson and I have been working with the packs where Omegas have gone missing, plus a few key informants, to put some pieces together. One of the Cleaners rescued a pair of Omegas from down south, including the fifteen-year-old girl everyone was in an uproar about a few months ago. Both had been drugged at some point along the way, though not continually. But Kalie is the only mated Omega we know of who's been taken."

"Because of the bond." Rebel frowned. "I can feel Charlotte wherever she goes because of our mating. They're drugging Kalie because they don't want to be found." He shook his head, his brow pulled down. "I didn't even know there was a way to hide the bond."

"Neither did anyone else, including Blaze." I nodded once as Rebel's surprised eyes met mine, letting him know I was just as shocked. No one had known until Kalie. No one had even guessed it was a possibility.

Rebel pulled out his cell phone, sending a quick message before looking back up at me. "I'm assuming you need help if you're bringing me in on this."

I nodded. "Jameson's on his way, but we'll need more manpower than the five of us. Gideon won't even count in the fight because his entire focus will be on getting Kalie to safety. We'll get Blaze to send a team of Cleaners as well, but again, their focus will be the Omega, as it should be. We need a handful of guys to have our backs."

"I figured as much."

The door opened, and Gates and Beast strolled through. Sibling shifters, both mated, the two would have looked exactly alike had it not been for the scars running down the side of Beast's face and the heavy beard he wore in contrast to his clean-shaven brother. My nerves settled just knowing they'd been the ones Rebel had called to help us. Gates was a powerful enforcer, trained in fighting styles that kept his enemies on their toes and made him nearly impossible to beat. Beast was…well, he was a beast. When he fought, he won. Unless it was against his brother. And both would understand the anxiousness Gideon felt. They were the perfect choice for the job.

"Everything okay in here?" Gates asked, eyeing the crowded office.

"Yeah," I replied. "Come in and shut the door."

Rebel steepled his fingers under his chin. "Gates and Beast, this is Alpha Killian and Gideon from the Southern Appalachia pack. Gentlemen, this is Gates and Beast. Two of my best."

"I see Zippo barbecued some shifter ass," Beast said, glaring at Killian and Gideon. "He one of yours?"

Killian nodded. "Yeah. Cahill's our packmate."

"He's out on the curb. You can pick him up when we're done here."

Gideon glared. "He's our pack, and now he can't even be in your building?"

"He hurt one of ours," I said, stepping closer and growling under my breath. "He's lucky I didn't skin him alive for touching her."

Beast gave me a confused look before refocusing on the two visitors, backing up my growl with one of his own.

"I apologize for my packmate," Killian said. "He was out of line to attack the woman the way he did."

I stepped back, catching Beast's eye and giving him a nod. "Fine. But keep him away from the denhouse. He's not welcome here."

Rebel, Beast, and Gates all stared at me, the pressure of their gazes harsh against my skin. But this was one time when I wouldn't let something like a secret keep me from saying my piece. Scarlett was my mate, and I would keep her safe by any means necessary.

Once I was sure my point had been made, I leaned against the wall and addressed the group.

"Gideon's mate is an Omega, and she's been kidnapped." I waited as Beast and Gates growled, that fact hitting too close to home for both of them as I knew it would. "Short version: some group is stealing Omegas and possibly drugging them. Whatever they're using is strong enough to dull the mating bond so they can't be tracked. We're making the assumption that it's the same group that tried to snatch Kaija back in October."

Gates growled. "Fuckers said their boss wanted to add her to his collection."

"Why only Omegas?" Beast asked, looking serious and pissed as hell. His stepdaughter was an Omega, the first that we knew of born to a human mother. He had just as much to lose, if not more, than his brother should these kidnappers get away with the shit they'd been doing.

"We know they keep them alive," I said, pushing off the wall to pace the length of the small room. "Cleaner Beelzebub happened to find his mate on that mission to rescue the fifteen-year-old Omega. The two women had been being held prisoner, and his mate said they called her the dud after they found out she was sterile."

"So they want to breed them." Rebel shook his head, a look of disgust on his face. I met Gates' furious stare and nodded. Gates' growl turned darker, louder. Beast joined him, the two filling the room with the threat of a battle no enemy would survive.

Rebel gave the two a dark look. "I know this is personal to you both, but we need to keep calm while we figure this shit out."

When Killian gave me a confused look, I shrugged. "Gates' mate is an Omega and was almost taken, and Beast's human mate just gave birth to an Omega shewolf."

"Well...fuck." Gideon shook his head, his shoulders sagging. "Blessings to you both, for the matings and the baby. We had hoped for the same, but..."

When he sagged, his emotions obviously holding back his words, Killian leaned forward. "They killed half our pack, focusing on our shewolves and our pups. They purposely destroyed our pack by using our weaknesses against us. We're a strongly bonded pack, an old one. We were able to fight back and kick them off our mountain, even taking a few out along the way. But it'll be decades before we can rebuild our numbers, and longer before those scars heal. I can only imagine the devastation these animals cause when they take on a smaller or younger pack."

I nodded, looking to Rebel. "They've decimated four packs that we know of, taking out every single member."

Rebel's eyes went wide. "Jesus, fuck." He sighed and ran a hand through his hair. "When will Jameson be here?"

"Within the hour."

"Can I see?" Gideon asked suddenly, surprising me, looking at Beast. "Do you have pictures of your daughter?"

Beast blinked twice, seeming startled by the request, but pulled his phone from his pocket. "Of course."

Gideon and Killian scrolled through the pictures, Gideon's face a mask of pain, Killian's almost furious.

"Kalie and I wanted to have pups right away. We spent her heat cycle away from the pack for some privacy, you know?" Gideon said, his voice harsh and filled with pain. "The fuckers who took her, they snuck into camp not long after we got back. They killed our packbrothers and sisters, our young ones. They took away a lot of our future as a family and a pack."

Killian handed the phone back to Beast, his eyes darkening and a low rumble sounding in his chest. "I want these fuckers dead for what they did."

"I understand that and will do whatever I can to help," Beast said, laying a hand on Gideon's shoulder. "Do you have a picture of your mate?"

"Of course." Gideon pulled his own phone from his pocket, scrolling through pics with a wistful smile on his face. "Here she is. My little firecracker."

My gut clenched at the nickname, my thoughts immediately going back to Scarlett, my own firecracker. Jesus, if she were in danger like Gideon's Kalie, I'd be a wreck. A violent, raging wreck ready to take on the world.

Gates took the phone first, smiling down at the picture. "She's lovely, Gideon."

I took my own look, nodding and passing the phone to Beast. "She's beautiful. We're going to do our best to find her."

Gideon sighed. "I just…I want her back. If I would have known—"

Beast's growl interrupted Gideon and had Killian jumping to his feet, ready to defend his packmate.

"Motherfucker." Beast swiped past a few more pictures. "I've seen her."

"What?" I stepped up behind him, looking at the pictures again. "When? Where?"

"February." Eyes wide, Beast looked up at his brother. "The

sick redhead I saw that day you arrived. The one Aaric's pack brought in."

"Are you sure?" Gates asked. "You only saw her for a minute and from far away. Are you positive it's her?"

"Absolutely," Beast said with a nod. "That scene has played out in my nightmares a million times, but she always ended up replaced with Calla."

"Who's Calla?" Gideon asked.

"My mate." Beast turned to Rebel, the two of them looking as if the pieces of some puzzle only they could see were suddenly coming together. "She was pregnant when I met her, and the father of the baby is the Beta of the local pack where she's from. I was doing recon on them as I planned how to get her out of town safely when I saw the redhead. Aaric's pack has your Kalie in North Dakota."

TEN

Scarlett

I PACED BEHIND THE bar, obsessively watching the clock, waiting for Shadow to come out of Rebel's office. I wasn't sure why, but I couldn't fight the need within me to stay close, to check up on him and make sure he was okay. To just be close to him.

"You're seriously stressed."

I spun, finding Julian sitting on one of the pleather barstools. He stared at me, his sunglass-covered eyes focused over my shoulder. Blinded in a car accident, if I remembered right. Sad, especially for such a young man.

I nodded, even though I knew he couldn't see me. "There's some scary people running around."

Julian shrugged. "So? You can handle yourself."

"What are you talking about?" I asked, raising my eyebrows.

Julian shook his head. "I'm blind, not oblivious. I know you can do things most people can't."

My mouth fell open, but the words wouldn't come. How did this boy know anything about me? Before I could answer him, a man walked into the denhouse. Tall, blond, and delicious, but with an air of anger about him. Dangerous, almost. Hot as fuck and pissed as hell, wrapped up in one pretty package.

"Where's Shadow?" he asked, his eyes barely pausing on me long enough to acknowledge my existence.

"That seems to be the question of the hour," I replied, pointing toward the back. The man glared at me before turning and heading toward Rebel's office. I huffed and grumbled under my breath, "Well, isn't he just Mr. Sunshine?"

Julian giggled. I rolled my eyes and went back to pacing the length of the bar, even more nervous now that tall, light, and deadly had joined my…whatever Shadow was. My nothing. My something. My possibility of something? Damn it, this red thread shit was confusing.

Minutes later, the sound of booted feet rushing toward the bar had me spinning on my heel. Shadow came around the corner of the hall first, his eyes roaming the room until they landed on me, took me in, practically caressed me from the opposite side of the room. My breath rushed out, and my back relaxed as the tension I'd been holding dissipated. He was safe. But oh, the serious expression, the way he looked at me. Like he needed me, like he wanted me. Like he'd been just as worried about me as I was about him.

Shadow hurried over, grabbing my arms gently and walking me backward until he had me pressed against the wall beside the bar. Covering me with his body.

"I have to go," he whispered, his lips so close, they nearly brushed my cheek. "I'll be back as soon as we get some shit settled, though. Maybe an hour."

"Okay." I nodded and swallowed hard, my insides tying themselves in a knot. Desire and denial raced through me, leaving me unsure of what to say next. Of what to do. Because I wanted to pull him closer, press my lips to his, and set us both aflame. But I also wanted to push him away, get him off me, and run.

Unaware of my inner turmoil, he stepped back and picked

up my hands, frowning at my burns again. "Will you be here when I get back?"

I shrugged, fighting to keep myself calm, to not let my confusion show. "I don't know. I was thinking of heading home once you..."

I trailed off, not wanting to admit that I was waiting to make sure he was okay. His slow, shy grin was proof that he knew what I'd left unsaid. And that he liked it.

Shadow reached into his pocket and pulled out a set of keys, removing a small ring from the rest.

"These are to my apartment upstairs." He placed the cold metal in my palm. "Second door on the left. Please just stay there. We've kicked the asshole who attacked you off property, but I'd feel better if I knew there was no way for him to come across you, just in case. I'll be back in like an hour, and then I'll take care of your burns, okay?"

My fingers curled around the key ring automatically, brushing his in the process. Oh, the jolt that small touch gave me. The way it sent sparklers of sensation shooting up my arm. I nodded, clutching the key ring, wishing he was staying with me for just a little bit longer. Still wanting to hide from him at the same time.

"Yeah," I whispered. "Okay."

"Good." He leaned forward and pressed his lips to my forehead, making a full-body shiver pass through me. "Try not to burn anything down while I'm gone."

I sighed, craving his lips elsewhere. "I make no promises."

He smirked as he backed away from me. "I wouldn't expect you to."

And then he left, following the other guys out the door without a look back. I was still staring after him like a lovesick puppy when Julian giggled again, drawing my attention to him instead of the unholy hotness of my red thread's ass in tight jeans.

"You like him," Julian singsonged.

"Shut it, kid."

He grinned and leaned toward me over the bar. "You lllloooovvveeeee him."

"Do not," I huffed, crossing my arms over my chest. The keys bit into my palm, reminding me of Shadow's touch, making my stomach clench with something warm and needful. Something almost strong enough to fight back the fear that left me cold.

Julian, being an annoying teenager, shook his head and kept picking at me. "You really lllliiiikkkkeeee him. You want to kkkiiiissssssss him."

"I'm so kicking your ass."

His grin only grew. "Yeah, because that would go over so well with your new boyfriend—kicking the ass of a blind kid. Sure, give that a try. Let's see how well it goes for you."

I glowered, really fucking irritated that my bitch glare had no effect on the kid. "You're a pain in the ass."

"I know, but I'm an observant pain in the ass, especially for someone who can't see." He sat back, his grin falling, his face becoming much more serious. More mature. "You like him and he likes you, but it's more than that. Just like how Rebel and my sister have more between them than a normal attraction. It's beyond love, like some kind of connection that the rest of us can sense in the air when you're in the same room together. Why are you pretending you don't feel it?"

The weight of Julian's words slammed into my chest. The bond between Shadow and me was growing even though I still wasn't sure if I wanted it to be there. Was that growth from real feelings, or was his wolf just trying harder and harder to sink his teeth into me, to force me to submit to this fated mate thing? And how would I know if Shadow really cared about me at all? Or if the red thread was all we had holding us together?

"You smell when you think," Julian said, yanking me right

out of my inner turmoil.

"Pardon?"

"You do. You smell like smoke when you think. It's different than most people...interesting."

I huffed. "You're a little crazy."

"No, I'm a little blunt. You smell like smoke when you think, and you burn people when you fight them."

Once again, my jaw fell open, unable to find words to refute his claims. I had a deep, illogical urge to tell him the truth, about witches and my powers, but I couldn't. It simply wasn't done. And yet...

"How do you know this stuff?"

"I'm blind, not deaf. And definitely not dumb." Julian smiled, all casual, as if he hadn't just called me out for being able to make flames flare from my skin. And for totally underestimating him. "You should probably go up to Shadow's place and grab a shower before he gets there. He might want you to smell prettier."

I shook my head, my voice soft and weak when I finally found it. "If he can't handle me smelling like smoke, he can't handle me at all."

His face scrunched up in question. "Who said he wants to handle you? Maybe he just wants to hang out with you."

"Somehow, I doubt it."

Julian shrugged and stood up, pulling his cane out from under the bar. "Not all guys want to own you, Smoky. Some just want to hang out around the person they find interesting, even if they may or may not smell like a chimney."

My mind swirled with indecision and confusion. I stared after him as he turned and walked out the front door, his words cutting straight through the chaos inside of me. That kid had unknowingly given me a place of calm to hold on to, a sense of rightness that hadn't been there before.

I fiddled with Shadow's keys, weighing them, weighing my

options at the same time. I could leave them here and go home. I could run back to my little rented house that I shared with my sister, then head for the bar to find someone to dance with, to make me forget. Or I could follow the thread wrapped around my heart, risking it all on a pull that only the Fates could have created. To stay or go, give in or surrender. To let the Fates lead the way or walk my own path.

Heart racing, stomach clenching, palms sweating, I sighed and headed for the door.

ELEVEN

Shadow

SIX HOURS.

That's how long it took me to get back to my apartment. Between phone calls to Blaze and Dante, learning what we could about Aaric's pack from Beast and Calla, and trying to keep Gideon and Cahill from going wolf and running their asses all the way to North Dakota, I was exhausted. And pissed. There was no way Scarlett had stayed. I'd told her I'd be back in one hour. Six was way more than one. She was finally starting to open up to me, to put her trust in me, and I'd broken that with a lie that wasn't actually a lie. More a really bad moment of timing.

Reaching up to grab the spare key off the top of the doorframe, I huffed and let loose a small growl. It was an uncontrollable response to the night, honestly. My mood had started turning south two hours into the meeting; at this point, it was completely soured. But when I opened the door, that quickly changed. I smelled Scarlett's smoky cool scent in my space and that alone calmed me more than all the pep talks and deep breathing could have. I liked smelling her in my den, liked how good it made me feel to know she had been here.

Or was still here.

The gentle sound of her breathing reached my ears, making my heart thump and my mood lighten. She'd *stayed*. How I'd gotten so lucky, I had no idea, but I wasn't passing this opportunity by. I closed the door carefully and hurried across the room, grinning when I saw her curled up in the corner of the couch like a cat. So pretty and sweet in her sleep.

Not wanting to wake her but also wanting her to be more comfortable, I gingerly picked her up and carried her to my bedroom. She could stay with me tonight, and maybe we could talk in the morning. At least that's what I hoped. A little time to get to know her before I had to leave for the next mission.

Once I had her in my bed and under my covers, I stood back and just watched her for a moment. Dark hair flowing down my pillow, those dyed bright ends like flames over the white cotton. Her even breathing as she rested, face relaxed and calm. So beautiful. So enticing. I wanted her to be mine more than I'd ever wanted anything, and her being in my apartment gave me real hope that our mating had a chance. That I had a chance.

Exhausted but almost giddy with relief, I made my way to the bathroom to get ready for bed. Or rather, sleep. With Scarlett in my bed, unbeknownst to her, I'd have to spend the night on my too-short couch. But the discomfort would be worth it. I just wanted her near me. Especially after the day I'd had. Watching Gideon break down over the loss of his mate had shattered something inside of me, made me desperate to protect Scarlett in a way I hadn't experienced before. Had she not been here, I probably would have ended up driving to her house. Tracking her. Needing to be sure she was safe.

Gideon knew his mate was not safe, and it had been killing him a little bit more every day as he waited for any piece of information on where she was being held… Would probably rip his heart apart these last few hours before we could get the right team in place to check out the latest lead.

Shaking off the memories of the past six hours, I hurried through a quick shower and brushed my teeth. I tossed on my favorite pair of sweats and, remembering Scarlett in my bed, tossed my T-shirt in the laundry basket. Hell, she seemed to like what she saw the night she brought me food. May as well work that to my advantage.

When I walked out of the bathroom, Scarlett was sitting up in the bed, pressing the blanket to her chest. Her hair sat atop her head in a mess of tangles, black, red, and orange all woven together into a fiery cloud. Her makeup had smudged a bit under her eyes, and her lids were half-closed in a sleepy stare. She'd never looked as beautiful or as tempting to me.

"Hi," I whispered.

"Hi." She looked around, bleary-eyed and confused. "Where am I?"

"My bedroom." I snorted a laugh when her eyes widened. "I figured you'd be more comfortable in here. I'm going to sleep on the couch."

"No, you can't do that." She jumped up, disentangling herself from my sheets. "That couch can't be comfortable. You should sleep in your bed. It's okay; I can go home."

"Scarlett, it's two o'clock in the morning. I'm not making you drive all the way to Downriver." I leaned against the wall, trying to look casual even as I fought the urge to cling to her. Damn, I did *not* want her to leave.

She cocked her head and gave me a look that should have warned me off, one filled with bricks and mortar and the possibility of walls going back up. The ones I thought I'd finally blasted through.

"I've been out well past two before."

I stood, unable to think of what to say to that. Of course she had. She wasn't helpless or on curfew; she could do what she wanted. And right then, it looked like she wanted to leave, which made my stomach sink and my mood drop right back into the darkness.

"Yeah," I said as I ran my hand over my hair, avoiding her eyes. "I understand that. If you want to leave, I can walk you to your car. But if you're trying to make me comfortable, you driving through the night won't do it. To be honest, I'll probably jump on my bike and follow you home."

She puffed up, looking ready for a fight until I held up a hand.

"Not because I think you can't make the trip, but because I'd want to be sure you arrived safely. If you left now and I stayed here, I'd end up worried and waiting for you to let me know you made it. Then I wouldn't be tired because of the anxiety. If I followed you, I'd end up driving back up here and being awake from the ride. So really, you leaving will just keep me up all night while me sleeping on the couch means I'd get to actually sleep."

We stood in the world's most awkward silence, eyes locked on one another, as I wished she would stay and she probably wondered how to bolt past me.

"Do you want me to stay?"

Her whisper nearly set my soul on fire. She had no clue how much I wanted her with me, no idea that I craved her the way I did. But I'd make sure that ended tonight.

I looked her right in the eyes and gave her a firm, "Yes."

No games, no bullshit, no lies. Just one sincere answer.

"Then I'll stay." She shrugged, playing casual, as if she hadn't just made me the happiest guy in the city. As if she hadn't just welcomed me through that thick wall of hers and given me such a gift. "But only if you stay with me."

"Of course. I'm not going anywhere tonight. I'll be right out on the—"

"No," she interrupted. "I mean, I'll stay...if you stay in here with me. I can't take your bed from you."

My mouth went dry. "You want to share a bed?"

Scarlett huffed, looking away. "Well, if you don't want to, then at least let me sleep—"

This time, it was my turn to interrupt. "I want to."

Eyes back on mine, she shrugged, looking so damn nervous even as she tried to play it cool. "So do."

Slow steps led me to her. "Are you sure?"

"Did I ask you?"

"Yeah," I replied, grinning. "You did."

"Then I'm sure." She stood up and crossed the room, heading for my chest of drawers. "I'll need a shirt to sleep in."

I licked my bottom lip, imaging her wearing something of mine, how the thin fabric would carry my scent and mark her as my own to the other men in the club. "Sure. Yeah."

She waited, a small smile on her lips, as I dug through a drawer for the right shirt. One that would be indelibly burned into my memory. I grabbed my favorite—soft cotton, black, well-worn—and handed it to her, our fingers touching for a brief moment. She smiled and hurried into the bathroom, presumably to change.

When she returned to the bedroom, she sat on the edge of the mattress, watching me and waiting. She looked so strong with her head up and eyes on mine, a warrior in my bed, in my shirt. There was no use doubting her sincerity even though I knew this was a big step for her. Hell, it was a giant leap for both of us, and we were just going to sleep.

I paused, frozen in place for a single moment, and then walked across the room. Finally heading toward her with cautious steps…always following her lead. Giving her the time to change her mind, not that I wanted her to. Not in the least.

The anticipation licked at me, crawled up my spine, and made me shiver. Scarlett watched me approach, her eyes intense, never faltering in her gaze. Every step made my heart beat a little faster, made my groin tighten a little more. The woman was going to kill me. From giving me the cold shoulder to sharing a bed with me, she'd knocked down every wall she had and opened herself up to me in a way I hadn't expected tonight. I had no idea how I'd get any rest with her right there next to me, but I was damn sure willing to try. Willing to stay up all night watching her sleep as well. Whatever it took to be with her.

When I reached the bed, Scarlett scooted across the mattress, holding up the covers for me. Inviting me in. My hands shook as I grabbed them, but I didn't pause. I slipped underneath, staying right on the edge of the mattress. Too afraid to move closer, and definitely too afraid to touch her.

"Shadow?" Her soft whisper stopped my whirlwind thoughts and gave me a point to focus on.

"Yeah?"

"Why'd that guy call you a mutt?"

I sighed as the rage I'd felt when Cahill spit that insult at me came rushing back. "Because he's kind of a jackass."

She shifted closer, her arm curled under the pillow her head rested on. "But why mutt? Is that a big insult in the shifter world?"

"Yeah, Scarlett," I said, my voice soft in the blackness. "It is."

"So what makes you a mutt?"

"I'm not…" I sighed again, my hand slipping down to the striations across my groin out of habit, hating to admit my secrets but refusing to lie to her. "I'm not purely a wolf shifter. My father was a wolf, but my mother isn't. She's—" another pause, another deep breath before I voiced the secret I'd held on to the longest "—a tiger shifter. A Borzohn or born wolf like Cahill looks down on Anbizens, or men who've been turned to shifters from human. They absolutely rage against shifters with mixed heritage like me. Cahill called me a mutt because he must have found out my background, and it was his way of trying to overpower me."

"Is it a secret?"

"Yeah, a big one. Rebel knows, and our Feral Breed president Blaze, but that's it. If the others found out, they might…" I trailed off, the thought making my stomach go sour. My brothers, the men I trusted with my life, may not feel the same way about me if they knew. And wasn't that just a kick in the balls.

"They might shun you," she whispered, sounding so scared and small, I knew the word meant something to her. Something deep and painful.

"Yeah. They might kick me out."

"I won't tell."

I smiled, my heart contracting at her innocent declaration. "I never thought you would."

She lay quiet and still for a few long moments, watching me. I stared right back, my wolf happy in my head, my tiger almost smiling. Our mate was in our den with us, staying through the night. We couldn't ask for anything more than that. Not yet.

"Shadow?"

"Yeah, Scarlett?"

"I'm glad you came back."

I exhaled forcefully, relaxing into my mattress and shifting just a little closer to her. "And I'm glad you stayed. Thank you for that."

She inched toward me, watching me. I didn't think she could actually see me in the dark, but my animal senses gave me terrific night vision. She stared at me as she approached, wary but confident at the same time. Her movements slow but steady. And when she touched me, when she finally brushed her hand against my arm, I gave in to my desires and wrapped myself around her. The world stood still while she snuggled into my chest and tangled her legs with mine, sighing when I encircled her in my arms and held her tight.

"This doesn't mean anything," she said, trying to sound all harsh and tough as she cuddled into me as if I was some kind of mostly human teddy bear.

"Nope," I said, my voice soft, my lips brushing the top of her head. "Doesn't mean a thing."

"We're friends. Friends cuddle."

I smirked. "Sure, I cuddle with Rebel all the time."

Silence…and then, "Really?"

"No, never."

"Too bad," she said with a sigh. "That'd be hot."

I chuckled and squeezed her tighter, wanting more of her, but grateful at the same time for having even a single moment to hold her. "Goodnight, Scarlett."

"Goodnight, Shadow."

And with my arms around my mate, it would be.

TWELVE

Scarlett

THE INFERNO CONSUMED ME, burned me from the inside out, the heat licking at my skin as I erupted in flames. Orange and blue, gold and red, they danced along my skin until every inch of me had been turned to ash. Until there was nothing left but soot.

Until the world went black.

I sat straight up in bed, my breath coming in gasps and my heart pounding. In that place between asleep and awake, I panicked, afraid of what I'd done...of who I'd been with. The room wasn't my own, the cotton sheets not what I would have chosen for my bed, and I was wearing only a T-shirt that was too big to be mine. For a brief moment, I worried that I'd gotten drunk and made a decision I'd regret. Something that would destroy the fragile connection I'd created with a particularly handsome man who had manners and a cutting sense of humor. One I'd only just let myself start to get to know.

But then the bed moved, and I ended up staring down at the man in question. Shadow rolled toward me, his face relaxed in sleep, curling his body around my hips and wrapping an arm over my thighs. Searching me out and calming me without conscious effort.

Asleep and unaware, he looked far too tempting for me to resist. Shaking, fingers curled in and almost afraid to make contact, I brought my hand to his face. I ran my knuckles over his eyebrows, along his chin, down his neck, relishing the tingles and sparks of recognition flying up my arm. This was him... my soul mate. The man the Fates decreed as perfect for me. A terrifying thought, but one that scared me less this morning than yesterday, and even less than the day before. Either the idea was growing on me or Shadow himself was.

I stared at the place where my skin met his, imagining that the bright red of the thread connecting us was visible in the early morning gray of his bedroom. It would glow, pulse, refuse to be ignored. Much like the man himself, who had captured my attention by doing nothing but being himself.

Truth be told, I was getting tired of trying to fight my connection to him.

Still, as nice as Shadow was, and as much as parts of me wanted him in my life, I had no idea if he felt the same. He could be attracted to me simply because his inner wolf told him to, or because his tiger side thought I'd birth strong kittens. Tigers didn't form packs like wolves did, a lesson remembered from high school biology. Would he even be able to bond with me the way the Fates expected? Would the man feel conflicted over the different needs of the animals within? Zuri and Phoenix seemed to really be in love, but that could be a fluke. Or Phoenix's wolf could be running the show in his mind. If I was going to give up control to be in a relationship with someone, I at least wanted to know they—the man, the wolf, and the tiger—were with me because they chose to be and they were committed to me. I didn't want him by my side because some ancient magick thought he should be, and I didn't want to be left behind because one part of him didn't feel the same attachment as another.

By the Goddess, my bond to Shadow was like trying to start a relationship with three people at once.

"You're thinking too much," Shadow murmured, his face buried in the pillows. He reached out and pulled me down, manhandling me until I was cuddled up against him once more. Facing him. Unable to escape. "What's got you all tied up inside?"

I huffed a laugh, thinking of the red thread between us. "You have no idea how close to the truth you are right now."

He lifted his head enough to peek at me with one eye. "Explain."

"Not now." I snuggled closer, breathing in the warm scent of him. "Right now, I want to lay here until I have to get out of your bed."

He ran a hand over my hip, making my body heat. "You don't have to get out of my bed at all if you don't want to."

"Yeah, I do." I tangled my legs with his, greedy for his touch, taking comfort from the way he surrounded me. "I've got a busy day today."

He hummed his understanding before tightening his hold on me. "Then give me a few thinking-free minutes. I can't rest when your thoughts are screaming."

"Okay," I laughed. "I'll give you ten minutes think-free, and then I have to get up."

"Deal." He sighed and held me close. What should have felt awkward or uncomfortable—the whole being in bed with a man I barely knew—was quite calming and comfortable. Right in a way that should have felt wrong. I lay in his arms, watching him, contemplating fate and life and control until his eyebrow wiggled.

"You're staring."

I bit my lip, fighting to hold back a giggle. "I'm not."

"You're totally staring." He poked me in the side, making me jump.

"Did you just try to tickle me? What are you, like ten?"

He opened his eyes to glare at me while smiling. "You're staring, and it's creepy."

"I'm not creepy."

"You're a little creepy."

I leaned up, resting my arm on his chest so I could look down at him. "You invited me to stay the night, to sleep in your bed. What does that make you?"

He shrugged, eyes closing, hand rubbing up and down my back. "Someone who digs your creepiness."

"You barely know my creepiness."

"You're my mate. I know enough."

I froze. Shadow opened his eyes and rearranged himself so we were lying side by side, staring at each other. Inches apart.

"Stop it," I whispered, my throat tightening as his words repeated over and over in my head.

"Why?"

"You don't know me."

"So let me get to know you."

"You wouldn't want to if it weren't for…" I couldn't say it, suddenly too tied up in knots to get my words out or be willing to admit my fears.

"You think I wouldn't be interested if you weren't my mate?"

I nodded, unable to speak.

"Not true." His words were strong, true, but not enough. Words would never be enough.

"How do you know?"

"I just do."

I sat up, pulling the blanket with me. "How can you be sure?"

"I just am."

"That's not really helpful."

He sighed, yanking me toward him and rolling me on top of him. "You are ridiculous, beautiful, funny, sarcastic, confident, strong, nurturing, and too fucking smart for your own good. And I like all of that, plus you're practically sex on legs. I like that, too. If you weren't my mate, I would have tried to get you into my bed. Period."

I pushed off his chest, my eyebrows furrowing. "Just your bed?"

His eyes met mine, suddenly wary. My stomach sank as a sense of doom flooded through me. Whatever he was about to say, I wouldn't like it. I could already feel the tension growing between us, pushing us apart.

"I don't... I've never really been in a relationship." He lifted his head, running his nose along my neck, clinging to me as if he knew I was about to run. "Tigers tend to be more solitary, but wolf shifters mate for life. I didn't ever want to risk committing to someone when I knew fate could change the game in the blink of an eye if my wolf side dominated my destiny. All my dating has been casual."

Change the game...casual...mate for life.

And there it was, my fear laid out in so few words.

Shadow had never dated, never committed to anyone, because of the Fates' pull on his animal sides. Three sides to one man, all battling for control at any given moment. How many women should the man have fallen in love with? How many times over however long he'd been alive had he denied his tiger side a natural attraction to someone because maybe, just maybe, the Fates would step in and plop someone into the wolf's path that they believed was right for him? Not right for the man or the tiger, but perfect for the wolf. Just the wolf.

"Oh." I pushed away from him, sick to my stomach.

"Scarlett, that's not to say—"

"No, I get it. I even kind of understand it." I rolled out of bed and grabbed my clothes from the floor, refusing to look him in the eye, giving in to my urge to flee. "I've got to get my day started."

"Scarlett, wait."

I paused at the doorway to the bathroom, keeping my back to him. "Really, Shadow, I get it. You've never had anything more than a hookup with a woman, but then I come along and all of a sudden you're supposed to get all forever and only with me. Maybe…depends on which side of you is in control at the moment."

"I—no—that's not—"

"Yeah, it is. That's exactly what this is." I hurried into the bathroom and shut the door. My eyes burned and my hands shook, sparks of heat tingling under my nails. Fate was a cruel bitch, but I wouldn't fall to her. Not this time, not with something as important as my heart…as Shadow's.

Running a hand through my hair and wiping off my smudged makeup, I shook my head. This was such a mess. Right as I was ready to let the Fates win, he throws out this game changer. I had no idea what to do next. Accept him and hope all three sides of him eventually accepted me? Give him a chance to break my heart? Or run for the fucking hills before the thread became too tight to escape…if it wasn't already.

I sighed, wiping away the single, tiny tear too persistent not to escape. I needed time, room to breathe, space to think, and I couldn't find it in his apartment…smelling like him, wearing his shirt.

I ripped the garment over my head, tears falling freely, my throat tight and my face burning. Damn it, dressing took way too long. Bra, shirt, pants…too long, too long, too long. I couldn't breathe, could hardly see. I needed to just go.

The second I was covered in my own clothing, I rushed out of the bathroom and into the living room. I had to leave before he pulled me back under his spell. Needed to go this very minute. That urge to escape completely overwhelming and unavoidable. Pure protection instinct, though whether I was protecting his heart or mine, I had no idea.

As soon as I grabbed my purse, I strode for the door, but Shadow blocked my way. Eyes flat, hair mussed and straggly, sweat pants low on those bitable hips, he looked as if he'd been worked over, like a man after a beating. And maybe he was... though the bruises I'd leave were buried too far inside to see.

"Talk to me," he said, his voice quiet, filled with hurt. My heart panged, but I couldn't falter. The longer I stayed, the smaller the apartment seemed, the harder it became to catch my breath. To keep my thoughts clear.

"I have to go." I tried to move past him, but he grabbed my arm. Loosely, not forcing, asking. Just one more thing about him that made me want to smack myself for not jumping at a chance to be with him. One more reminder of how much he deserved someone to truly care about him. Even if that person wasn't me.

"Scarlett, please wait."

I shook my head and pulled my arm from his grasp, swallowing hard as my eyes burned again. "No, I don't think that'd be a good idea right now."

He let me go, stepping back, giving me space. I walked past him, desperate to go, just as desperate to stay. Buried in doubt and confusion.

"Am I going to see you later?"

My stomach dropped and my heart cracked. I wanted to say yes, to exchange numbers and talk about how we'd meet up later, but I couldn't. I couldn't lie to him or give him false hope when I had no idea if I'd be able to be near him without freaking out anytime soon.

Unable and unwilling to back down, I opened the door, avoiding his eyes. "Doubt it. I have plans tonight."

"Plans." The ice in his voice stopped me, almost forced me to turn around. "You mean a date."

"I mean plans, which are none of your business." I strode down the hall, my steps quick, running away from what he represented. Escaping something I'd never realized I wanted before it wrecked me…or I wrecked it.

When I reached the stairs, I tossed out a casual, "Thanks for letting me stay."

His reply came harsh and in a tone I'd never once heard from him. Not one he'd ever used on me. One filled with anger. One that told me how much I'd just hurt him. "Yeah, right. Anytime."

And then he slammed the door.

THIRTEEN

Shadow

"SHIT."

My legs locked, feet planted to the floor as I growled, fighting back my inner tiger who was trying his damnedest to take control. He wanted to shift, to chase Scarlett, to hunt her down and claim her whether she liked it or not. He was the side of me that had to be contained. The one that could do some serious damage if he got out. The one I fought against the hardest.

My wolf remained quiet, barely a presence in my mind. Hiding. Our mate had refused us…again.

I ran my fingers through my hair, pulling and fisting the long strands as my heart crumbled in my chest. What had I said this time? What had I done? We'd finally been alone together, made physical contact, had a conversation. She'd let me in. But without warning, she'd built those walls back up faster than I could stop her, higher and more guarded than before. She'd completely locked me out. Why was that girl always hiding from me?

The answers didn't magically appear, which meant I only had one option. I'd have to ask her. I chuffed a sad laugh and shook my head at that idea. Right, because she was always so willing to talk to me. The woman had the whole unattainable and uninterested thing down to a science, one my brain simply couldn't wrap around. She'd gone from soft and snuggling to hard and indifferent before my very eyes. And I had no clue why.

Fuck me, I needed to clear my head.

I crept into my bedroom, holding my breath, almost afraid of what her scent would do to me. My mate had spent the night in my bed, in my shirt, and my room was going to be filled with her enticing smell. It was going to hurt to breathe. Hurt deep and hard. I needed to just man up and take it in. Suffer through it. Rip it off like a Band-Aid.

So I did.

The snarl that left my lips as the cool fire scent of her swept into my lungs was louder and stronger than my wolf ones. More roar than growl. Oh, our little firecracker had truly enticed the beast. The one who didn't mate for life, who wasn't tied to her by fate.

"Easy, kitty," I whispered into the empty room, hard and aching from nothing more than Scarlett's smell, the pain in my chest overriding the need in my groin. But she'd been pressed up against me all night, been soft and sweet and *there*. And goddamn, she'd been so warm.

But she'd left me in the cold, alone, and unsure of what to do next.

Before I could clear my mind enough to think things through, my phone pealed and jittered across the nightstand. I dropped my head and sighed, honestly almost grateful for the distraction, knowing there was no way it was the person I most wanted to talk to.

"Yeah?" I said as soon as I swiped to accept the call.

"We need to meet up." Jameson's growl came through the line, the sounds of the denhouse in the background. "Get your ass downstairs pronto."

"On it." I hung up and tossed the phone on the bed, glaring at the device. Useless piece of plastic. I didn't have Scarlett's phone number to call or text her and attempt a conversation. I had no idea how to get in touch with her. And I'd be an idiot to ask Phoenix for the information. If she wasn't ready to tell anyone I was her mate, I'd honor that. I had enough secrets of my own, I could respect hers. Even if it did add a heaping pile of salt to my wounds.

Surrendering to the fact that I'd have to wait on her to reach out to me, I made my way into the bathroom for a quick shower. Planning, riding, fighting, saving the Omegas...those things needed to be my focus. At least for today. At least until my inner beast took over and tracked her ass down.

FOURTEEN

"FUCK FUCK FUCK FUCKITY fuck." I slammed my hand against the steering wheel, sending sparks flying as my emotions took control. I'd never been more furious with myself. What was I thinking? Why didn't I stay with Shadow and give myself a few minutes to calm down so we could talk about things like adults? Why did I have to be such a bitch?

"Yeah, right. Anytime."

How much damage must I have done to make him talk to me like that? Not so much his words, which could be taken different ways. No, the sickening guilt in my stomach was caused by the tone he used. The anger and hurt that came through. The flatness, the clipped words. And oh Goddess, the door slam.

What had I done?

"Are you planning on coming inside, or should I bring your breakfast out here?" Amber stood on the porch, arms crossed, giving me her sarcastic calling-you-a-dumbass face. And I was; I absolutely was a dumbass for this one. Still, I flipped her off and grabbed my keys, trudging past her when I reached the porch.

"Don't ask me about my night. You don't want to know."

"Oooh." Amber followed me inside, positively giddy at my foul mood. "If you tell me I don't want to know, that means I do. I really, really do. So spill."

I shook my head. "You're going to call me immature."

"No, I won't." Her innocent act came on strong, all high-pitched voice and wide eyes. But I knew her better than that. Way better.

I snorted, pointing at her as I scrunched up my face. "Yes, you will."

She rolled her eyes and tossed up her hands. "Fine, I will. But why don't you get it over with? You know you'll talk eventually."

I plopped on the couch and let my head fall back. I couldn't relax, couldn't even close my eyes without seeing the pained expression on Shadow's face. Hear the echo of his door slamming. My entire stomach was one giant knot, twisting and expanding, making me nauseous. Making me sick with myself for what I'd done. Stupid hot shifters with red threads wrapped all around them…and the idiotic ways I reacted to them.

Amber sat next to me, so I rolled my head in her direction. Her light eyes met mine, calm and patient as the air around us. For all her bluster, she was my friend, one-third of our sisterhood along with Zuri. If ever there was someone I could trust, it was my sisters. I fought for them, supported them, kept secrets for them. I left my home and my coven and the only life I'd ever known for them. I could tell either one of them anything, especially Amber, the little mother. The responsible one. She'd listen, and she'd tell me what to do. How to fix things if I could.

Besides, she'd know soon enough anyway if she didn't already. Privacy and air witch didn't really go together.

I blinked, my eyes burning with tears threatening once again to fall. "I was with Shadow last night."

"About damn time," she said with a grin.

I shook my head, ending up staring at the ceiling. "Not *with him* with him. We were supposed to talk and he was late, so I slept at his place. Totally PG."

"Oh," Amber said, frowning. "Well, that sucks, but it's not that big of an issue unless he couldn't get it up."

I squeezed my eyes closed and rubbed my temples, groaning. "I can't even talk to you right now. This is about so much more than sex."

"Fine, fine, I won't talk about his malfunctioning penis. So you spent the night with him, sans sex. So what?"

"So," I said, drawing out the word. "I screwed up."

She stared at me, her face going from slightly mocking to serious. Amber was a lot of things, and not all of them good, but she was my sister to the end. It may have taken her a few minutes, but by the look on her face, she finally recognized how upset I was. How much pain I was in. How messed up I felt inside.

"You freaked out," she murmured, her eyes soft and without a hint of judgment. Only understanding. Knowing.

I sighed, staring at the ceiling once more. "I didn't freak out…completely."

"Ah, so a minor freak-out. Just enough to put a huge speed bump in the middle of your future." She snuggled close and tugged my hair out of my face. "Scarlett, he's a nice guy."

I turned toward her, that knot in my stomach growing bigger with every second, forcing me to fight back the sick just to keep talking. "Amber, he's never had a girlfriend."

She paused, taking that in, but then she shrugged. "So what? That's kind of admirable considering the whole mating dilemma."

"Sure, admirable." I wiped my eyes, punishing the traitorous tears making their escape. "Until he realizes he's only with me because his—" I paused, biting back the truth about his inner beasts, knowing she'd figure it out but not wanting to betray his trust "—animal side wants him to be. Not his human one."

"You're amazing, Scar. Any man would be lucky to have you in his life."

I shook my head, my voice rough when I finally spoke. "I'm not. I'm not anything special, but he is. He's so fucking amazing. He'll stay with me because the Fates tell his wolf to. But what if that's not enough? What if I give myself to him and he…"

I cried unknowingly, tears of fire running down my face, dropping to my lap, singeing the fabric. As Amber shushed me and rubbed her hand over my hair, trying to calm the swirling emotions I couldn't control, I took a deep breath and released the negative energy within me into the world, praying to the Goddess to make it go away.

"He'll stay until he decides to check out greener pastures because mine isn't the right color green or the right kind of pasture. He'll stay for a while, but the different sides of his nature may not always agree, and then he'll cast me out."

"Scarlett, come on." Amber gripped my shoulder, still cuddling against my back. "He's your red thread. He'd probably rather chew off his own arm than cheat on you."

"You don't know that." I sat up, turning and tucking one leg underneath me to face her. "He didn't pick me, the Fates did. He knows absolutely nothing about me. His wolf could be all, *Ooooh, a mate*, while he's all, *Fuck, a mate*."

Amber held my gaze, her face giving nothing away as she said, "You know that's not what's going on here. You're just scared."

I rolled my eyes, visions of Shadow and wolf packs and lone tigers berating my mind. "I am not."

"Are too. Shadow wouldn't cheat on you. Fidelity and caring for their mate are programmed into their little wolfy brains. He's practically a monk because he's been waiting for you."

I cocked my head and pursed my lips. "I said he didn't date, not that he didn't fuck around."

Her eyes widened before she pulled her face back into a frown. "So what? As you would probably say if you weren't so torn up and emotional, his dick may be used but it can be refurbished, plus his heart is showroom shiny."

I snorted a laugh, her words making my stomach flutter. Not that I was ready to believe them. Not that I was willing to surrender to hope.

"You have no idea what you're saying."

"No, I'm right, but you don't want to admit it. He's a nice guy, a hot one, and he's got eyes only for you. So what if the red thread kicked off that attraction? Can you honestly say you wouldn't have noticed him without that connection? Can you honestly say if he walked up to you in a bar, you wouldn't have given him the time of day?" She leaned closer, pressing her forehead against mine and dropping her voice to a whisper. "Give the man a chance—an honest to Goddess chance— before you write him off, Scar. He deserves that much."

I swallowed hard, peering back at her as my heart began to race. "What if I'm not what he wants?"

Amber frowned, obviously thinking about that, before she shrugged. "Then you toss him to the other animals and head back into the woods for seconds. Like Goldilocks, but with shifter dick instead of porridge."

I huffed even as I fought back a laugh. "Amber, be serious."

"Scarlett," she mimicked. "I'm totally serious. I hadn't believed in the whole red thread legend until Zuri met Phoenix. But seeing them together, feeling the aura of love around them…that bond is real. It's beautiful and amazing. I want that for you. Be brave, Smoky."

I pursed my lips, ready to argue. But I couldn't. I didn't want to. Shadow had grown on me with his manners and his kindness. He'd pulled that red thread tight and wasn't letting go. And really, I no longer wanted him to. Amber was right, if I'd met him any other way, I'd probably have thrown myself at him.

I sighed and dropped my head. "You're right."

Her lips turned up in a big, broad smile. "I really like hearing those words from you."

"Shut up." I pushed her shoulder. She laughed, coming back to place her forehead against mine once more, her eyes serious.

"He's not the coven," she said in a quiet voice, making the knot in my stomach turn to lead. "He's not Bethesda or any of the other women who turned their backs on us. He's a good man, I can feel it. You'll be so happy with him."

I squeezed my eyes closed, the ache in my heart deep and strong. "What if he—"

"He won't," she interrupted. "He won't become them. He won't pretend to love you then turn his back on you. He won't let one side of him betray the bond between you."

She drew closer, her lips right against my ear as she whispered, "He won't shun you."

The lead knot in my stomach unfurled, spinning and twirling but finally giving me enough room to breathe. I inhaled deeply. The air seeped into my lungs, refreshing my very soul, forcing out the negative with its cool, clean purity. Leaving me with nothing but the simple truth.

I wanted to have Shadow in my life, to explore our connection and learn about him. To give him a chance.

"I need to talk to him."

Amber shrugged. "So call him."

I froze, staring at her with wide eyes. "I...don't know his number."

"Phoenix will know it."

"I don't think he's told Phoenix about us." I bit my lip, uncertainty stealing my will to be brave. I didn't want to spill his secrets, even though they were mine as well. It just didn't feel as if it was my place to tell one of his denmates about us. Even if said denmate was my future brother-in-law.

"I'll wait," I said, knowing my decision affected him and not wanting to hurt him again. "If he's not at the denhouse tonight, I'll track him down. He was pretty pissed when I left, and I'd rather give him time to cool off."

Amber eyed me, probably wishing she could just call him and talk to him on my behalf. Domineering little witch. I gave her a hug and a whispered "Thanks, sis" before leaving her on the couch. I needed to clean up and find some new clothes. My shirt and jeans had new burn holes in them from my tears. I fingered one as I walked across the room, the black edges making me frown. I'd never cried tears of fire before.

"So," Amber asked as I turned to walk upstairs. "How bad was your freak-out?"

I flinched, flamey tears forgotten as Shadow's words echoed in my mind.

"Yeah, right. Anytime."

"Bad enough for him to slam the door in my face."

Amber's eyes went wide. "Ouch. You might want to make that apology in private. Wearing lingerie. Carrying a giant pan of lasagna."

I huffed and headed up the stairs. "Yeah, that makes sense. 'Sorry for being a bitch. Have some pasta and me.'"

"Hey, no man can turn it down," she hollered up the stairs.

"Please, I've been turned down plenty."

"I meant the lasagna!"

I TOOK A SIP of my drink and scanned the bar again. Still no Shadow. My stomach pitched as I berated myself for not having the guts to just track down his phone number, but I'd been too nervous. Too afraid he wouldn't answer or wouldn't be willing

to talk to me if he did. I'd waited all day at the denhouse for
him but to no avail. So I came to the bar down the street where
I knew the guys hung out, dragging Amber with me. And then
I lurked on the edge of the dance floor like a creeper. Waiting.

I hated waiting.

"Hey, Scarlett."

I spun, my deep need to see Shadow overriding the reality
of the voice behind me. Because it wasn't him—not even
close. Too weak, too soft, too…wrong. Way too wrong. Dull
Doug stood with two drinks in his hands, smiling down at
me, wearing pleated khakis and a pale blue Polo shirt. Bland,
boring, and fifteen different levels of wrong. What had I been
thinking?

My smile felt plastic, my eyes darting behind him of their
own volition. "Hey, Doug. How are you?"

"Good." He grinned, really putting out the plastic Ken-doll
vibe, making me recoil a few inches. "I'm glad I ran into you.
I was thinking about heading out to a brewpub in Novi for
dinner tomorrow night. Was wondering if you'd want to come
along?"

He handed me a drink just as I spotted a head of dark hair
over the crowd around the bar. Long, shiny hair pulled into
a low ponytail. Hair I knew smelled like some kind of deep,
masculine soap. That felt good pressed against my cheek.

Hair that belonged to the only man I wanted to talk to.

I shook my head, trying my best to smile politely at Doug
while keeping an eye on Shadow. "I'm sorry, but no. I'm not
available."

"That's okay. Maybe next weekend." He reached out and
grabbed my arm, directing me closer. Sparks fired under my
skin, heating me in a way Doug would never understand. That
he could never know about.

"No, I really can't." I finally got a clear view of Shadow as
the crowd parted, just in time to see him walking across the

dance floor. Away from me. I took a step in his direction but stopped, frozen, stomach dropping all the way to the floor.

Some blonde walked right behind my Shadow, following him too closely to be a stranger.

"So what do you think?"

"What?" I asked, really getting sick of Dull Doug getting in my way. I needed to see what was happening across the bar. Shadow wouldn't have hooked up with someone already. I'd slept in his bed last night, plus he was my mate, my fated red thread. He wouldn't...would he?

"Are you feeling okay?" Doug ducked down, blocking my view as he gave me a quizzical look. But I had no answer to give because Shadow had just walked out the back door, the girl right by his side. Together. My heart paused, my breathing stopped, and the fire inside of me died, leaving me cold and alone.

Oh hell, they left *together*.

"Scarlett? What's wrong with you?"

"Nothing. I'm fine," I whispered. But I wasn't fine. My heart was breaking from the loss of something I hadn't known I truly wanted, my red thread strangling me. I wasn't even close to fine.

I turned away from the door, the image of Shadow's back slipping outside with blondie right on his ass burned into my memory. He left with someone else. A woman. Someone who wasn't me. The pain turned my skin cold, my blood to ice. Stopped my heart and froze it in place. Or at least that's how it felt. He'd shunned me for someone else.

"What's going on, Scarlett?" Doug stared down at me, eyes a little angry, mouth hard. Not that I cared. Not anymore.

I shook my head and handed him back the drink he'd given me. Over it...over him...over the games and the fear and the distance I purposely kept between my red thread and me. I was over everything.

"I'm really not interested in you like that, Doug."

Before he could do much more than drop his jaw, I rushed across the floor, the icy sting of hurt quickly turning to anger. My blood boiled, my hands growing hot and uncomfortable as I lost control of my power. I needed to leave, to run. To get out. Before I exposed myself or hurt someone. Before I exploded.

"Where are you going?" Amber asked when I grabbed my purse from the seat next to her.

"Home."

"Why?" She raised her eyebrows, obviously confused as she watched me dig for my keys.

"Did you not see that?" I yelled, not caring who heard me. "He was here. He didn't come over to me, didn't talk to me, and then he left with someone else."

Amber's brow furrowed. "What are you talking about?"

"Shadow...he left with some" —I waved my hand and made a face— "blond chick."

Amber's laugh sounded loud and bright, attracting more attention than I wanted and making the heat of my anger burn hotter.

I shook my head and turned for the door. "Thanks for the support, sis."

"You are an idiot," she said, rushing to my side and falling into step with me.

"What? How am I the idiot?"

"That was Kaija."

I froze, hand on the door, brow pulled down tight. "No, it wasn't."

"Yes, it was. One of the guys was calling for Shadow, but he wasn't answering his phone. Kaija came to bring Shadow back to the denhouse. She was talking to me when he walked in, and they left together."

"No way." I shook my head. "I would have recognized her. I *know* Kaija."

"Well, apparently you don't know her ass, because that's the blonde who just walked out with Shadow." Amber grimaced. "He looked a little pissed off, by the way."

"Why?" I stared at her as she raised her eyebrows. Thinking back to the moment when I saw him, I tried to imagine what would have pissed him off. I'd been on the dance floor, waiting, watching. I'd looked past Dull Doug to…

"Shit." Pain rushed through me as my fingers sparked, pops of light dropping between the door and me.

"Yeah," Amber said with a nod, glancing toward the falling embers. "*Shit* about covers it."

"Not helping, sister-mine." I huffed and stepped outside, clenching my hands into fists, looking toward the denhouse.

Amber snapped her fingers in my face, making me jump. "You want my help? Here it is—grow up, get your act together, and go to his apartment."

"For what? You just said—"

A cold wind blew past us, one not fitting with the heat of the evening air. A sure sign Amber was calling on her own magickal element.

"I don't care what I just said." Her hair caught in a circle of wind wrapping around her, lifting it, making her seem as if she stood in the center of a tornado. And maybe she did. Maybe she was struggling with control as much as I was. Between her wind and the sparks falling from my fingers, we'd certainly have trouble explaining ourselves should someone see us.

Before anyone else walked out of the bar, I grabbed her arm and dragged her down the road toward the only safe space I could think of. The only place where we could go full witch without earning much more than a raised eyebrow, or a growl.

"We need to get off the street," I hissed, clenching my hands to try to contain the sparks.

"We need to get you to Shadow."

I huffed, my stomach tight. "Why are you pushing this

so much? It's my future, not yours. Besides, you said someone called him. Last time he had to meet up with these guys, he was gone for hours."

Amber shook her head, the action making dirt from the sidewalk lift into the vortex of her personal wind. "Not this time. He'll be there in a few minutes. You have to go to him."

"Amber—"

"Don't Amber me." She stopped, head high and eyes unfocused, wind blowing hard against me as she shook. "Dammit, Scarlett, quit acting like a child and do something the right way for once. You only have a few hours before…"

The wind died, and Amber sagged, almost physically shrinking in front of my eyes.

"Amber?"

She shook her head, her eyes tired and sad when they met mine. "If you wait, you'll run out of time. I've done my best, Scarlett, but I can't keep playing against their destiny. Go now…before it's too late."

FIFTEEN

"WE RIDE AT SEVEN." Jameson grabbed his beer, cracking his neck before downing the bottle.

"Sounds good. Gideon will be glad to hear it." I stretched as I stood, tired but too revved up for sleep. We'd been working out the North Dakota mission finalization all day. I'd taken one break, a quick walk over to the bar down the street to track down Scarlett, but I'd been called back to go over the ride details. Good thing, too... I'd found Scarlett all right. At the bar, on the dance floor, talking to that preppy bastard I'd seen her with a few times. Maybe it was a good thing Kaija had come to bring me back. I'd been as close to losing control of my animal side as I'd ever been watching her smile at that guy. She pushed me away and ran to someone else, someone almost the complete opposite of me. A human. If that was what she wanted, I'd have to let her go. I couldn't be human, couldn't hide my animal sides or desires. I couldn't be what she seemed to want.

Leaving her wasn't what I really wanted to do, but it was inevitable. I'd be heading back to Chicago after this mission anyway. One reclaiming wouldn't solve the case, and my time was better served there. Or at least, that's what I let myself believe.

"Think Beast minds that he's not going?" Jameson asked.

I shrugged, shaking off my depressing thoughts. "Nah, I'd bet he gets it. Besides, I don't think he wants to leave little Aliyana."

The Feral Breed crew we'd selected would be headed to North Dakota in the morning to infiltrate the pack where we believed Kalie was being held. We'd gotten every bit of information we could about the group of shifters from Beast and Calla, but we couldn't let him in on the extraction. He was too closely connected, what with the way the pack Beta—the father of the daughter Beast saw as his own—had screwed over Beast's mate. Beast would be sitting this one out. Luckily, Gates knew exactly where the pack had set up camp. He'd lead us in once we got to the city where we'd met Calla, and we had a solid team set up to assist. We'd strategized, planned, and researched terrain maps a thousand times over the last two days. It was time to attack.

We were bringing home Kalie the Omega, no matter what… At least one set of mates would get a shot at their happily ever after.

Jameson led the way down the back hall. "Between what Beast says and the fact that Gideon can't feel their connection, my guess is they've kept this Omega drugged up hard."

"Agreed," I said. "There's no way she's fully conscious, even during the times when Gideon *can* feel her."

"And with the news out of Louisiana that the kidnappers were looking to breed the Omegas…" He trailed off, glaring at the implication he refused to voice. A ball of anger exploded in my chest, making me growl low. Lord have mercy, just the thought made me sick. I wanted to rip these fuckers apart with my bare hands.

I nodded once, not needing to say what we both knew we

could be walking into. "Gideon will kill them."

"Or die trying." Jameson sighed. "I know you're not mated, but that bond is a tough one to control, if not impossible. If they've done anything to her, if he smells her blood or—" he paused, curling up his lip in obvious disgust "—the scent of sex anywhere near her, Gideon's going to lose it. He could cost us the mission and men's lives trying to defend her."

"True." I swallowed hard, trying not to think of Scarlett and what I would do if someone hurt her. If someone dared to touch her against her will. The tiger inside of me roared in my head, knowing exactly what he'd do if anyone touched her. How he'd pay them back for her pain. "We'll have to keep him out of the first wave for sure, though it's going to be hard to control him. All three of those mountain men are itching for a fight already."

"We're going to have to make them obey, even if that means Alpha-ordering their asses." He bumped my fist as we reached the main room of the denhouse. "Get some rest. We get to brawl with some big-bads tomorrow night and maybe save a damsel in distress. Don't forget your stethoscope, Doc."

"Yeah, right." I gave him a head nod before he turned and headed for the door, probably planning to go back to his hotel and prep for tomorrow. I wanted to follow him, not to his hotel, just out the door. Down the street. Back to the bar. I wanted to find Scarlett, but knowing my luck, she'd be out with Mr. Prepster. And I...well, I'd probably hurt even more if I were to see that. Time for me to go back to my apartment and hunker down for the night, no matter how much my inner animals wanted to sniff out their mate. My human side couldn't handle the let down again.

I climbed the back stairs at a slow pace, my insides tied up in knots. Between the mission and the shit with Scarlett, my thoughts were stuck on mates, women, and the bond between the shifter and their fated match. What the hell would I do if

Scarlett disappeared, especially when she seemed one step away from refusing our bond? Without a claiming bite, I wouldn't be able to track her down if she needed me. I wouldn't be able to sense her. Not that the bond was helping Gideon much. The fuckers who'd taken his mate and killed half his pack knew how to block the connection between the two, and that was some scary shit.

Mated Omegas had been deemed safe when we first started investigating the kidnappings. Not because of the protection of their packs, but because they'd easily be found through that bond. No one who wanted to stay hidden would risk such a thing.

But a kidnapper who could block that connection? When word got out about this, there'd be outcries and mass exoduses as mated pairs left their packs to hide in the deepest wilderness they could find. Not a good situation for the pair, the pack they left behind, or those of us tasked with keeping them safe while not intruding on their lives. The hysteria would make it easier for Omegas to vanish, and we'd be left trying to piece together how and where and why.

The apartment was dark when I entered, but I didn't turn on a light. Didn't need to. My heightened animal senses meant my eyes quickly adapted to the low light. Besides, I didn't want to see the evidence of this morning's disaster. The messy bed, the sheets tangled, the hole behind the door where I'd punched through the drywall. It was bad enough the place still smelled of her, of smoke and flowers. It almost hurt to breathe.

Knowing I needed to be up early, I slunk off to the bathroom. I would wash the day away with a hot shower, wash the scent of Scarlett from my skin. Not that it would matter— that scent was embedded in my memories, her essence burned into my soul. I could scrub for days and I'd never be rid of her.

Once under the water, the thoughts of Scarlett didn't disappear. In fact, the memories of last night played in my mind, growing louder and brighter on each repeat. Of holding her tightly against my body as she rested. Of the way she would sigh and wiggle closer in her sleep. I'd barely closed my eyes for most of the night, but it hadn't mattered. I'd had my mate in my arms—sleep was an interruption.

Thinking of her warm weight against me, of the feel of her skin against mine, I reached down and grabbed my aching cock. I'd been almost continually hard since I met her, since I felt that bond. And no matter how much I jerked off, I couldn't find the relief I needed. Logically, I knew it was the mating frenzy, the urge to claim her with my body and my bite, but that didn't make dealing with the constant arousal any easier. My dick was chafed and my balls were bluer than a Smurf's, but nothing helped. My hand was no substitute for what I really craved.

Sighing, growling, I ran my fist from base to tip. Slow... easy. But Scarlett wouldn't be slow or easy with me. She had spunk, fire. She'd own my cock with a look if I gave her a chance. And I would. I'd give her every chance if she'd let me.

I sped up my movements, pulling harder, tugging and rubbing and teasing the head on every other pass. My breath increased with the speed of my hand, my heart pounding in my chest. Fuck, the water running over me reminded me of how hot her body could be, how her skin burned against mine. I turned up the temperature, nearly scalding myself, but the heat felt good flowing down my chest and abs, over my cock, down my thighs. The burn felt right.

Grunting, I spread my legs wider, the telltale tingle of an orgasm starting low in my belly. Just a little more, a few more strokes, a spray of hot water running down my legs. One hand on the wall, one working my cock, I growled and grunted and sighed my way to completion, nearly roaring as I came in heavy spurts that disappeared instantly down the drain.

When I was as sated as I could get on my own, I leaned my forehead against the tile, trying to catch my breath and clear my head. Damn, that girl was going to break me one way or the other. Break my heart and my cock. Though really, if she outright refused me, it might be a broken soul. Which was a really fucking depressing thought and not what I needed to focus on considering all that needed to get done.

Sighing, I stepped out of the shower, fully intending to dry off and crawl into bed. The bed that probably still smelled like Scarlett. Just a little extra torture for the night. I was still naked when someone knocked at my door, their scent hidden under the steam and the smell of my soap. Figuring it had to be Jameson coming to go over more details, I dropped my towel. *Motherfucker.* We'd been at it all day. Couldn't we take a few hours off?

Growling in frustration, I yanked on my sweat pants and hurried down the hall.

"I swear to Christ, Jameson, I'm not in the mood—"

All my words, my anger, and frustration died the second I opened the door. My voice changed from a deep, growly, irritated tone to a breathy sigh as I said the only word I could think of.

"Scarlett."

She looked so nervous standing at my door—shy, almost. Not at all the sassy woman I was used to seeing. This one had dropped her walls completely, leaving her vulnerable and open. She made me want to hold her, protect her, ease her anxiety. But I stood stock-still, staring, waiting for whatever she was here to accomplish. Preparing for the worst.

"I probably should have called." Her smile was small and forced, unable to reach her pretty green eyes as they tracked over my bare chest and up to my wet hair. "Oh God, you're busy. I'm sorry. I can go."

"No." I reached for her, unable to resist, shivering as our skin met. Fuck, this girl would destroy me, and I'd enjoy every second as I went down in flames.

She didn't pull away when I circled her wrist with my fingers, didn't retreat, so I carefully pulled her inside my apartment and closed the door behind her.

"I'm glad you're here."

She glanced past me into the living room, still cautious and obviously uncomfortable. "I didn't want to interrupt."

"You're never an interruption." I grinned as she gave me a sarcastic smirk, looking pointedly at the water running over my shoulders from my soaked hair. "Okay, fine. You're never an *unwanted* interruption."

She looked toward the living room again, then nodded. "If you're sure."

"I'm sure."

Silence fell over us, the energy turning awkward. I had no idea what to say or why she was in my apartment. Not that I wanted her to leave. But still, what was this? Why did she come here? And why was I suddenly so nervous?

"I'm sorry about this morning," Scarlett finally whispered, pulling out the big guns with a sad expression on her face and a tiny pout on her lips. "I didn't have a date tonight, I only said I had plans because I needed time to think." She shuffled her feet, biting that pouty lip, staring at the floor, making me nearly shake with my need to comfort her. "I can't always think clearly when I'm around you."

She looked up at me, eyes so big and bright. Lips so pink. I could barely resist her. And yet...

"So then why were you at the bar with that guy?"

"You mean Dull Doug?"

I had to bite back my smirk...*dull indeed*. "Is that the preppy fucker I saw you talking to? It's not the first time I've seen you with him."

"We've hung out a few times, but tonight wasn't about him." Looking up, she speared me with her gaze, her obvious honesty. "He walked up and started talking to me. That was not planned at all. I was there alone, looking for you, hoping you'd come so I could talk to *you*. I didn't have your phone number so I couldn't call, and I was too afraid of having to explain our whole" —she scrunched her nose and waved her hands around— "situation to ask Phoenix for it. But then…"

"What?" I asked when she didn't continue.

"You left," she whispered. "I saw you leave with…Kaija."

So many pieces fell together when she whispered Kaija's name—the nervousness, the fear, the looking over my shoulder when she arrived.

"You didn't know it was Kaija." I inched closer when she nodded, stalking her, making her my prey. "Were you jealous?"

Her eyes flashed, a bit of annoyance there. "Were you jealous when you saw me with Doug?"

"Yes."

She opened her mouth to speak but stopped, probably having no retort for my honest and straightforward answer. Of course I was jealous. I saw no shame in admitting it. Though I did like the fact that she was jealous as well. It gave me hope, a little boost of confidence that she might give me some kind of chance.

I inched closer, desperate to bask in her heat, craving her scent. "And if I hadn't come in the bar at all?"

She kept her eyes on mine, red and orange sparks slowly dancing with the green. Something magical and stunning, unique to her. "I would've come here to find you."

I stepped closer, bodies brushing, forcing her to retreat. A soft growl escaped as my wolf pushed against my mind. Ready for his mate, ready to claim.

"You were hunting me?"

She licked her lips when her back hit the wall, trapped. "Yes."

My growl deepened, rumbled from deep within me, a sound of want and need and lust. This woman did me in, made me weak and strong at the same time, made me want things I hadn't expected or planned on. Made me needy for her.

"You've got me," I whispered, leaning over her, running my nose along her cheek. "What are you going to do now?"

Scarlett made a little gasping sound, one I wanted to hear again and again. "Shadow."

"Yes?" I breathed her in, scented her, tasted her on the air.

She gripped my arms, her hands so hot they burned. "I don't want to hurt you."

"Then don't." I dragged my lips along her jaw, to her ear, nuzzling her. My body pressing into hers. Hard against soft, warm against fire. Perfect.

Scarlett whimpered as I bit her earlobe. "Sometimes, my fire, I can't control it. It's been hard lately."

"Me, too. But there's burn ointment in the closet." I licked my way down her neck, barely touching her with my tongue, teasing myself with her taste. And oh, what a taste it was. Spicy, sweet… Mine.

She clung to me, almost kneading my arms, her breaths fast and the scent of her arousal building. "I'm serious."

"So am I."

I lunged, giving in to my desire, pressing my lips to hers as I grabbed her ass and lifted. She wrapped her legs around my waist, using the leverage between me and the wall to edge herself higher, pull me closer. There was no delay in the kiss, no warm-up or tentativeness. As soon as our lips touched, our mouths were open, our tongues dancing together in a routine that could have been choreographed over lifetimes. But it was no fair give-and-take. She owned my mouth, controlling me, kissing me with a passion I'd never experienced before. And I loved it.

Goddamn, my girl could kiss.

I pressed my hips into hers, needing more, wanting to give her everything, to make her scream. To make her mine.

She wrapped her legs around me tighter, her heels on my ass, clinging to me through every stroke of my tongue against hers. But when she started to move, writhing against me, burning me up as she practically danced against my cock, I knew we had to stop. Fuck, I wanted her body, but I wanted *her* more, her heart and soul, her everything. I needed to make her open up to me. I needed to know she'd stay for more than just a few hours.

I pulled back from the kiss with two small nibbles to that plump lower lip. "You can't keep running away from us."

She swallowed hard, her eyes all lust-blown and wide. "I…I know."

"Is this it?" I kissed her again, unable to stop myself, craving one more taste. "Are you accepting us as a possibility?"

Her chest flushed, the red climbing, capturing my eyes. "I don't… I can't keep hurting you. But I'm scared. "

I pulled back, cocking my head. "Of what?"

"Of giving myself to you, and—" she closed her eyes, hiding once more "—and you throwing me away."

I rubbed my nose on hers, waiting for her to open those jade eyes again before sucking her bottom lip between my teeth with a growl. She groaned, her hips jerking against where I was so hard for her.

"You're my mate," I said once I'd released her lip. "The only one I get. My wolf wants you. My tiger is ready to claim you as his own, too. The bastard is obsessed with making you his."

"And what about you?"

"What about me?" I asked, grinding into her.

"Shit." She gasped and gripped my arms tighter. "What does the man want?"

I smirked and lifted her, lining up her sweet pussy with my aching cock. "What do you think? Do you think I only want this? That I just want to get inside you?"

She shook her head. "I don't know."

"Yes, you do." I leaned closer, kissing her deep and hard

before pulling back and placing my forehead against hers. "Scarlett, if that was all I wanted, I would have tried last night. You're more than a one-night kind of girl to me. I want lots of nights with you…years of nights. I want forever."

Her lips turned up—just the corners—in a sexy half smile. "Forever's a long time."

"It is, which is why we'll take it one night at a time." I leaned in, giving her a small kiss, barely a brush of my tongue on hers. "One hour. One minute. However slow we need to go. Until I get you to realize I'm not going anywhere."

"Shadow—"

"You're it for me, Sparky. Not because of fate or some kind of magic tying us together. Because I choose you…because I want you. You're mine and I'm yours, if you want me."

She kept her eyes on mine as I gave her a second to think. Not kissing, not moving, not pressing. Just she and I staring each other down. Waiting each other out. Opening myself to her in the most honest way I knew how.

And then she set me on fire with a whispered, "Yes."

"Yeah?" My cheeks burned as my smile grew.

"Yeah, of course I want you." She pulled me closer, shifted her hips to rub herself along my hard length, made me sigh and growl as she teased my cock through our clothes. "I need you, Shadow. All of you."

"So have me." I attacked her mouth and thrust against her, making her gasp as my hardness pressed into just the right spot. She liked that, so I did it again. And again. I kept doing it, kissing her hard, rubbing on her, squeezing her ass with both hands.

On a particularly rough thrust, one that made her head fall back and a nasty curse fall from her lips, she grabbed my bare shoulder. I hissed as the heat of her palm seared my skin.

Scarlett jerked back, seeming to recede into herself. "I'm sorry. I'm so sorry."

I shook my head, holding her eyes as I brought her hand back to my shoulder. Sighing through the burn of her skin on mine. "Set the whole place on fire, just touch me."

She resisted, curling her fingers against my skin and looking at me with what had to be regret. "But I could hurt you, or cause—"

"Don't care," I interrupted, pressing myself against her swollen pussy again just to see the flash of heat burn through her eyes. "Burn me, bite me, claw me…just let me make you feel good."

"Jesus." She writhed against me, her eyes nearly rolling back as she bit her lip. "I don't want to hurt you."

"You won't." I spun us around, carrying her, heading for the bedroom as she clung to me. "But even if you did, it wouldn't matter. I want to feel all of you against me. Right now."

"I don't know…" She shook her head and tried to look down, but I growled sharply. Her head popped back up and her eyes met mine.

"Scarlett, when was the last time you were able to get lost during sex?" I laid her down on my bed, crawling on top of her, not letting her go. "How long has it been since you could really let go and just come without worrying about fire or flames or burns?"

She stared, wide-eyed, cheeks dark. "I…don't remember."

"Oh, baby." I pulled her closer, gentling my kiss, sucking that bottom lip into my mouth as my hands massaged her ass. "Let me make you feel good. Give up on that holding yourself back thing and just let me take care of you."

"I want you to," she said as she tilted her head back. I latched on to her neck, sucking and biting my way from the top to the curve of her shoulder. Fuck, I was so hard, so desperate for her. Desperate for more sensation. The pre-come causing wet spots on the inside of my sweats, the heat of Scarlett's pussy through the worn fabric, the way her body curved into mine. I wanted her. Wanted to make her shiver and scream and gasp with my fingers or mouth. And, oh God, someday soon I wanted to bury myself inside her. Wanted to own that pussy and show her how much pleasure I could give her if she'd just let go. If she'd just give me a chance.

And then she did.

"Shadow, please."

SIXTEEN

Scarlett

OH HELL, I WAS in a very naughty version of Heaven. The way this man manipulated my body and made me want to crawl all over him with his words was irresistible. And his strength. He'd walked with purpose while holding me, carrying me through his apartment as if I weighed nothing. I'd never been manhandled by a guy before, but I liked it.

"Shadow," I whispered as he pressed me into the mattress. He growled a response, his mouth too busy treating my neck to some serious attention to form words. Attention that made me shake and squirm and want to feel that tongue elsewhere. "Please."

"Scarlett."

I shivered, the rumble in his voice making me gasp. Making me wet. Making me need.

"Yes." I arched into him, not sure what I was begging for, but wanting more. More touch, more sensation. My body burned from the inside out, pulsing with want, setting off fireworks inside of me. The only thing keeping me from bursting into flames was the man on top of me, licking my throat, biting me. Oh the Goddess, the biting.

Shadow groaned and shifted lower, keeping his mouth on my skin as he passed my collarbone. "My beasts can smell you, can tell how aroused you are. It's so delicious."

His hands found my breasts, making me writhe and moan as he massaged and kneaded the heavy flesh, as he teased my nipples.

"Shadow," I groaned, lost in sensation, unsure whether to beg him to stop or to keep going. To work harder. To make me scream.

He licked a path up my neck and pressed his lips against mine for a soft kiss. "Do you want me to stop?"

"No, but—"

He kissed me again, swallowing my words before pulling back and leaning his forehead against mine. "I want you naked in my bed, Scarlett. I want to taste you and tease you and make you come. Your smell is driving me crazy. Let me press my face against that sweet pussy and eat you up. I want to taste you so bad right now. That's *all* I want." He shook his head and chuckled. "Well, to be honest, I'd really like to fuck you six ways from Sunday, but I know it's too soon for that."

I grinned, biting my lip and shaking my head.

He sighed and kissed me again, gentler this time, softer. "If you don't want me to do anything, I won't. We can kiss and cuddle and fall asleep together again. I'll be a perfect gentleman. But if you want me the way I want you, then let me take off your clothes. Because putting my mouth on you is all I can think about."

I groaned. "Jesus, Shadow. You barely talk to me for days, show up in those fucking sweat pants, and then you lay all this dirtiness on me."

He shrugged, giving me a charming, boyish grin. "What can I say? I like to let people know what I want." He rolled to the side, placing his hand on my stomach. "And I want you." He slid his fingers under the waistband of my jeans, teasing my stomach, making me want to crawl right out of my own skin. "Naked." Lower, to the edge of my panties, sliding back and forth across my overheated skin. "In my bed."

He stared—his hand in my pants and his body pressed along the side of mine—while I worried. What if I hurt him? What if the fire within burned him? In the past, I'd never been able to tell someone about what could happen or why, which had made me hold back. A lot. The secret of our coven had always trumped their safety. But I wouldn't have to hide with Shadow. He knew my secret, and he hadn't run away in fear. He knew and wanted to touch me anyway... And damn was that attractive.

Throwing caution to the wind and hoping he knew when to back off if things got hot, I smiled and lifted my hips. "So what's stopping you?"

He smirked and slid his hand all the way into my pants. "Not a fucking thing."

His lips met mine once more, and his fingers began a slow, torturous massage over my panties. Pressing against my clit, sliding along each side of me. Teasing me brutally. I tried to lift my legs, to spread them, but my pants were too tight and his thick arm in the waistband wasn't helping.

"Stop," I said, pulling away from him as my frustration mounted.

He jumped back, eyes wide. "What's wrong?"

"You said you wanted me naked." I flicked my hand, indicating the clothing I still wore. "This is definitely not naked."

He grinned and shook his head. "No, that's definitely not naked."

I unsnapped my jeans and pulled the zipper down, keeping my eyes on his. Once loose, I lifted my legs straight up in the air and pulled the waistband over my hips.

"Want to give me a hand?"

He swallowed, his eyes tracking from my hips to my ankles. "Yes."

Hands soft, he placed my ankles on his shoulder and slid his hands to my hips. He tugged my jeans off slowly, reverently, running a hand over every inch of skin he bared. My panties came next. I shivered at the gentle way his fingers dragged the black lace down my legs, at the look of concentration on his face as his eyes followed their path. Black on tan, lace against muscle, sexy against strong. And then bare. He smiled and leaned in to kiss my knee as he tossed my clothes to the floor.

"Come here," he whispered, holding out a hand. I took it without hesitation, no longer fearing anything when it came to this man. I put my trust in him to take care of me, to treat me right, to be the person I knew him to be. To be mine.

He pulled me to a sitting position with my legs spread on either side of his. Watching me, staring at where I was swollen and wet for him. I leaned back, bracing my weight on one hand and letting the other trail along my inner thigh. Letting my fingers tease between my lips. Sliding two just inside.

Shadow licked his lips and moaned, a frenzied look in his eyes. "So fucking pretty."

He grabbed the bottom hem of my T-shirt, never looking away, sure and solid and totally in the moment. I lifted my arms, and he pushed my shirt up and over my head, leaving me in only a black lace bra. Before he could try, I reached behind me and unhooked the back, pulling the straps down and tossing it with the rest of my things, leaving me naked in Shadow's bed. Completely vulnerable and exposed. Legs spread, arms back, nothing left to the imagination. With him staring at me like I was the best thing he'd ever seen.

"Your turn," I whispered.

Shadow slid his hands up from my hips, running softly over my waist and ribcage, cupping my breasts and flicking his thumbs against my nipples. I let my head fall back, pushing into his hands, so turned on I could hardly breathe.

His eyes dark and a low growl vibrating through the room, he leaned forward to place a kiss to the swell of each breast before running his lips up my sternum, licking across my collarbone, and finally biting, kissing, and sucking on my neck. Good graces, the man had a neck fetish, and I loved it.

"You're ridiculously beautiful," he whispered into my skin, making me grin.

"And you're still wearing clothes. I don't really want to be naked all alone."

Shadow didn't hesitate. He stood and dropped his sweat pants—the only clothes he wore, apparently—standing naked before me in under a second. Naked and hard. So damn hard. And patterned.

"Stripes," I whispered, bringing my fingers to the striations across his groin. Light, barely visible, they captured my attention. The slight texture of them made me run my fingers over them again and again, the placement keeping my attention on his thighs, his hips, his cock.

He shivered and made a mewing sound as I teased the lines once more. "Birthmark."

I leaned forward, kissing the darkest stripe, the one that wrapped right over his thick cock and across his hipbone at an angle. "They're beautiful."

"You're beautiful."

While I eyed all he had to offer, he crawled over top of me, pushing me back and demanding my gaze. He let his whole body touch mine, joining us from chest to feet, even wrapping his arms under my shoulders to hold me to him. My soul settled as his body engulfed mine. It made me feel small and cared for, cherished even, a totally new sensation for me.

With a small smile, he leaned down, touching his lips to mine once more. Desperation growing, I slid my tongue into his mouth and curled my fingers in his hair. Directing him.

Leading the kiss. He groaned and sucked on my bottom lip for a moment before he pulled back, moving down my body. Taking his own path.

His lips blazed a trail from my neck to my collarbone, choosing to follow the curve of my breast lower, sucking my nipple between his teeth and giving it a small bite that made me gasp and arch into him. Once more, a final nibble, and then lower still, his hands kneading my hips as his lips and tongue teased their way to my belly button.

Down again, biting over my stomach, moaning and groaning and growling and driving me mad. When he reached my hips, he licked across the expanse—one bone to the other— before looping his arms under my thighs and pulling me down the bed.

"Shadow," I said, giggling. He hummed and kissed along the seam between my thigh and my stomach, licking a path down. I kept my hands in his hair, not guiding, just holding on. Following along, massaging his scalp, and tugging softly as he used his mouth to tease me. To drive me wild. To ramp up the expectation and desire.

And then I died a thousand deaths as he placed his lips around my clit and suckled me.

Sparks flew, though I couldn't tell if they were in my mind or real. If actual sparks erupted from my fingers, Shadow didn't seem to notice or care. He sucked and licked my little nub with a vengeance, never holding back, attacking me like it was his job.

When he wrapped his lips over his teeth and bit down on my clit, causing a rush of sensation throughout my entire body, my legs clenched, my head tilted back, and I groaned. Loud.

Shadow gripped me harder, pulling me tighter to him and pressing his tongue against me. Over and over he licked and sucked, pushing me higher, relentlessly teasing me. And when I couldn't take it anymore, when I sat on that edge of pleasure and pain that always came right before I broke apart, he used his teeth again and shattered the tenuous hold I had on reality. I trembled and stuttered, swearing, biting my lip, and trying to curl my body in on itself, but Shadow held me still, pulling me through, making that pleasure last. Making it the best orgasm I'd ever had.

When I finally had enough control over myself to act, I grabbed his hair and pulled him up my body. Kissing him deeply, tasting myself on his lips as his body fitted to mine.

"Want you to come, too," I murmured, moving to his neck. He had such a neck fetish; I knew it had to go deeper than just a want to give pleasure. I took a chance that he liked the same treatment, and I bit him…hard. He jerked and made a noise that sounded animalistic and dangerous, more roar than growl, more jungle than forest. I liked it. Liked that he wasn't quite human. Liked that I was able to entice all three sides of him at once.

I bit him again, not breaking skin, but sucking hard enough to leave a mark. To mark him as mine. He thrust against me, sliding through my soaking wet pussy, never inside but so damn close. Bumping my clit on every push forward, making me shiver at the sensation.

"You're so fucking hot." He groaned and dropped his head to my shoulder. "Your hands are going to set me on fire."

"I don't know whether to thank you or apologize." I clutched at him, loving the feel of his body against mine.

"Maybe a little of both." He huffed a laugh that mingled into a groan. "Jesus, Scarlett. Don't stop touching me. Please. I'm not going to last."

I squeezed my legs around his hips and thrust back against him, teasing him, giving him enough pressure to get off.

"Just let go, Shadow."

He shook his head, growling deeply.

Knowing he needed a little more, a tiny push, I lifted my

head to his ear and gripped his shoulders, burning him with my palms as I whispered, "Come on me, Shadow. I want you to mark me."

His body stiffened as a deep snarl ripped from his throat. Pure animal, nothing human about the sound. Body tense and face screwed up tight, he gave two more pumps before he came, decorating my stomach with the evidence of his pleasure as he shivered and pinched his eyes closed. I couldn't look away, amazed by the expression of pained pleasure on his face. Falling deeper under his spell as he let me see him like this. So raw. So desperate.

"Fuck, Scarlett," he groaned as he finally opened his eyes. "You can't say stuff like that to me."

I giggled and ran my hands over his shoulders. "Why not?"

"The beasts like it too much." He looked up at me, all blissed-out eyes and a lazy smile. "I'd hate to have you think of me as a two-pump chump."

"Hmmm." I slid down the bed, curling around him. "I wouldn't worry about that."

"No?" he asked as he wiped down my stomach with a tissue from the nightstand. "And why's that?"

"Because you can always make it up to me with your mouth."

He chuckled, tossing the tissue toward the trash can and wrapping his arms around me, cuddling us closer. We lay in silence, enjoying the warmth, relaxing into sleep. Until I ran my hands over his back and he flinched.

My eyes popped open, and I stretched to see the damage. Two dark marks, one on each shoulder blade. Hand marks.

"I burned you."

He shook his head. "It's fine."

I tried to push away, my heart racing and my stomach clenching, but he refused to let me go, hanging on to me with an iron grip.

"Scarlett, don't." He waited until I held still, then brought his face close and stared into my eyes. "It's absolutely nothing compared to what we shared. I liked making you come, and I liked coming all over you." He leaned down and gave me a tiny kiss. "I really liked that." He grinned and I rolled my eyes.

"I wasn't running," I whispered. "I was just going to grab that burn ointment you love to threaten me with."

"Oh, okay." He shook his head, smiling, eyes dark and locked on mine. "I don't want any medicine. I actually like the feel of them."

"You like it?"

He shrugged. "Kind of feels like you branded me or something. You marked me. They're a badge of honor."

"Seriously?"

He held my gaze, bold as day as he stated, "I earned those burns. I want them to scar me."

I grinned and shook my head. "You're crazy."

"And you're in bed with me. What does that say about you?" He chuckled as I smacked his arm, pulling me tighter and nuzzling into my neck. We lay curled around each other, warm and comfortable once more. Quiet and at peace.

But then it was his turn to break the silence.

"I have to leave first thing in the morning." He kept his arms wrapped around me as I tried to pull back, refusing to let me free.

"Where are you going?"

"North Dakota," he said, his eyes soft and sorry as they looked into mine. "It's for business. It hasn't been planned for long; we only finalized the trip this evening."

I watched him, waiting, feeling the secrets he kept like a tension between us. "Business?"

He paused, eyes wary, his body language telling me so much more than words. "I have a job to do out there. One I can't really tell you about."

A job…nothing more, nothing less. Damn, I didn't need to know all the details, but something about the way he spoke, about the tone in his voice and the stiffness of his words, set off alarms in my head.

"Is it dangerous?" I whispered, clinging to his shoulders.

He steeled me with his gaze, silent and stoic, and I knew my answer. He wouldn't lie to me and tell me no, but he also wouldn't scare me by saying yes. So he stared, and I stared back. Understanding. Accepting. Hating that he would put himself in such a position but knowing it was part of who he was. Part of his breed and his family of Feral Breed shifters. Something he could no more give up that I could being a witch.

I closed my eyes and leaned my head against his chest. Clutching him. "Be careful, okay?"

"I'll do my best." He nodded once, slowly, cradling me as he kissed the top of my head. "I'll come home to you, Firecracker."

SEVENTEEN

Shadow

WE RODE THROUGH SOME nowhere town in North Dakota long past sunset. The darkness had an oppressive vibe to it, a weight, as if the night was smothering the land. No bright moon in the sky due to the phase of the month and a lack of streetlights put us in the pitch, but I didn't mind. We'd come to work, to hunt and fight. For us, the darkness was a blessing, especially with our animal sides much closer to the surface than we'd normally let them be. We needed their ears and eyes, their sense of smell and their instincts, if we were going to pull off this mission. No more holding back.

We had a fleet of motorcycles ridden by Feral Breed members, a war wagon full of mountain shifters, a set of Cleaners coming for backup from Chicago, and a man practically foaming at the mouth to find his mate, all ready to go.

I'd been thinking about Scarlett the entire trip, too distracted by the memories of her heat and her taste to notice the scenery flying by. Her curves beat out any rolling hills, her spicy skin better than anything on the menus of the diners we'd stopped at. The long ride gave me hours to settle in to those thoughts, to thoroughly investigate every moment of the night before. Her breathy sighs. The feel of her legs wrapping around me. The way her hair glowed like the end of a cigarette when she came. And her mouth, her words. Calling my name, asking for more, saying "please" and "mark me" as I thrust against her. The woman was a firecracker—strong and bright, beautiful and dangerous as all hell—and I would stay bathed in the glow of her if she'd let me. I wouldn't stifle her, I'd let her fly and just enjoy the show, because deep down, I knew she'd come back to me. We may not have exchanged mating bites, but we'd bonded. She was mine, and I'd honor that to my last breath.

The ache of riding with a hard-on was a price I willingly paid to remember every moment of the night before. But as I pulled behind a roadside motel with my brothers, that changed. I needed to focus on the task at hand. The fight we were about to kick off. I needed to get down to business.

"I can feel her," Gideon said, nearly shaking as he hopped out of the SUV to stand between Cahill and Killian. Obviously fighting his urge to go to her…to run. "She's still fuzzy, but it's stronger here. We're *so* close."

Jameson stepped in front of him. "We *are* close, but you need to wait."

"I'm fucking tired of waiting," Gideon snapped, his canines descending. The man was over the edge, ready to lose complete control to his wolf and his need to protect their mate. When I thought of my Scarlett being in the same situation as his Kalie, I understood his desperation. I had no idea how the man was still standing after all the months of not knowing where she was or if she was okay. If he'd ever see her again. And now, when his mate was close enough to feel even through the haze of drugs the kidnappers had to be keeping her under, he'd have to sit back and wait more. Brutal.

"We're all tired of waiting," Killian said, echoing his packmate. "I say we go get her now." He crossed his arms and gave a solid Alpha stare, ready to fight. Killian O'Shea was a big man—huge, really. Tall and broad with arms as thick as tree branches, he exuded strength and power. But so did Jameson, who looked about ready to bash the other wolf's head in. Time to intervene.

"The Cleaners are coming tonight." I stretched, cracking my neck, and nodded at Killian. "Your pack, Rebel, and Gates need to stay put so someone's here to meet them. Phoenix, Jameson, and I are going to do a little recon before things kick off."

Gideon snarled, his shoulders hunching and fur sprouting along his arms. "I don't want to be held back."

I growled a warning, my one and only. "If we go in without knowing what the situation is, they could kill her. If we go in without backup, they could kill us all. We wait for the Cleaners, and we check things out from a distance. If she's in immediate danger, we'll act accordingly. Otherwise, everyone needs to chill the fuck out." I held his Alpha, nodding deeply, more of a bow, in a move that showed respect. "We're getting her back, but we have to do it right. I will not let you lose more pack members tonight, Alpha. You have my word."

Killian's glare broke, his face losing color. He'd lost a lot recently, as an Alpha and a man. But he was fair and kind, he loved his pack more than anything except maybe his mate. He'd never do anything that would harm a single one of them, which was why I knew he'd back down if I reminded him of the danger Kalie was in.

Finally, Killian nodded. "We stick to the plan, Gideon. These men are going to help us save Kalie, and we need to listen to them, no matter how much it kills us to."

Gideon's growl morphed into a sound like a whimper. "But I can *feel* her."

Cahill put an arm around him, pulling him into his side. "We'll get her back soon. And then we'll kill those bastards for touching her in the first place. And for murdering my sisters."

I locked my eyes on the desperate shifter, keeping my face flat and expressionless. Worrying about his ability to think logically in the face of what we were sure to find. All three of the Appalachian shifters were dangerous to our mission: Killian had an ax to grind because of losing the battle to keep his pack safe, Gideon had a mate in danger and would do anything to get her back, and Cahill…apparently he'd lost sisters in the attack. Lost family. The level of pain and fury the men had to be feeling would feed their wolves, make them lose focus, make them a liability instead of an asset. Unless we kept them on a short leash.

Rebel, Gates, and Phoenix had turned away, probably feeling the same pang I did when I thought about being in Gideon's shoes. But I held strong, faced down the man and the agony of his fear. Keeping my thoughts pinpointed on Gideon and Kalie. We had a mission to do, and it wouldn't help anyone for me to be distracted by my Scarlett. Not when there was so much at stake. Not if I wanted to be of any use during the fight that was sure to come.

Scarlett was a distraction I craved, but one I couldn't allow to take over.

"If you can feel her, then she can feel you. She knows you're coming for her," Jameson said. I turned and cocked my head. Those words didn't seem like something an unmated shifter would say. Jameson sounded…mated. Experienced. "Send her good emotions, safe ones, something for her to hold on to even if they've still got her drugged. That's your job for right now. You give her mental strength, and we'll go check out what's happening."

Gideon frowned, his face pained. His packmates edged closer to him, supporting him, offering what they could. These coming hours would probably be the worst for the mated shifter, be harder than any of the others simply because she was so close. This night would last a lifetime for him.

Jameson stepped right up to Gideon, face-to-face, voice rough and emotion clear as he whispered, "If I have to wear my cell phone on a collar, I will. If she's in trouble, we'll call you. If we see them touch her, we'll break through the doors. If she's in danger, we'll bust her out. I swear to you, we won't let them hurt her once we get her in our sights. We won't leave her behind, and we won't stop searching until we find her. You're going home with your mate."

Gideon blinked twice then nodded, his eyes more red than normal. Even in the low light of the parking lot, I could see him tearing up. His pain ate at me, made me lose focus because it could so easily be mine. My bond with Scarlett was already the best thing that had ever happened to me, the most intense emotional connection I'd ever known. But it was also my biggest weakness. I'd do anything for her, anything to keep her safe. And that made her a powerful weapon against me. Just like Kalie was for Gideon.

The mountain shifters disappeared into one of the cheap motel rooms we'd rented, hunkering down for the next few hours of torturous waiting. Our Feral Breed team followed Jameson and me around the corner of the building to the edge of the woods.

"Time to four-paw it," Phoenix said once we reached a spot deep within the tree line. He stripped off his clothes, placing them on a branch for when we came back. "How are you going to carry your phone, Jameson?"

The big man shrugged as he pushed his jeans over his hips. "In my mouth I guess."

I shook my head. "You'll slobber all over it."

"Good thing my case is waterproof." He smirked as he set his phone down where he could easily grab it in wolf form.

"Waterproof," I snorted as I pulled my T-shirt over my head. "You better hope it's wolf-proof."

The deep, dangerous sound of Phoenix's growl interrupted

our easy laughter.

"What the fuck are those?" he spat, charging toward me.

"What?" I asked.

He plowed into me, shoving my shoulder while twisting my body so he could see my back. "Are you fucking around with Scarlett?"

My stomach sank as I met Jameson's questioning eyes. Fuck, this was so not the time. I'd almost forgotten about the burns she'd left on my shoulder blades. Hiding the subtle tiger stripes on my groin had become ingrained over the years, and the bite she'd given me was small enough to look like a bruise or a hickey. But the two handprints seared into my back were new, large, like upside down wings on my shoulders. They were also very, very telling.

Pulling from Phoenix's hold, I held my head high. "It's not your business, man."

"Not my business?" Phoenix pushed me again, making me stumble and snarl. "She's like a sister to me. What the fuck are you doing screwing around with her?"

Rebel snorted a sarcastic laugh. "You're about to get your ass kicked, Shadow."

"Pretty sure Beast'll be taking a piece of your hide when you get back as well. If there's any left." Gates smirked and stood beside Rebel, the two watching, letting Phoenix and me work out our own shit.

Jameson leaned back against a tree, arms crossed, also watching. Knowing. And suddenly I sensed it—the man had to have a mate. I knew it like I knew my own mating bond. Why he was keeping it quiet was his business, same as why I hadn't wanted to tell the guys about Scarlett and me. But there was no doubt in my mind he'd found his fated match.

"You guys might want to ease up," Jameson said, giving me a smirk. "I'm pretty sure our Shadow isn't the hit-it-and-quit-it type anymore. Not when the girl has ties to his den. Especially not when the girl is a witch and can set his dick on fire if she chose to."

"True that." I gave him a nod before turning back to face the angry Phoenix. "It's not your concern."

"Fuck you," he spat. "Scarlett is my business."

"No, she's not." I crossed my arms, keeping the claws that had pushed through my fingertips from showing. I didn't want to fight my den brother, but I wouldn't let him come at me and not defend myself. I understood his concern, even liked it considering the situation, but I wouldn't let him win just because he cared for my mate like a brother. "You need to back the fuck up. She's my business, my concern. Mine."

That final word came out on a roar, not a growl or a wolf snarl. My tiger had staked his claim, and he refused to back down to a weaker species.

Phoenix's eyes went wide. "What the hell did you just say?"

"Guys." Rebel stepped between us, ever the voice of reason when things got a little too heated. Too bad I was past reason. I'd suffered through thinking my mate had refused me, I wasn't going to deny her or let these guys think they had any say in my relationship with her. She was *my* mate. Mine. Not theirs.

Phoenix inched closer, pointing his thick finger in my face. "I can't believe you'd do this, man. She's family. You don't get to fuck with my family."

I glared at him, making sure to let my animals peek through my human eyes. Both of them. "I said back up, and I meant it. My relationship with Scarlett is just that, mine."

Phoenix growled, forcing Rebel to grab him by the chest as he lunged for me. "You think you can take her to bed and what, claim some kind of ownership? She's practically my sister."

"No," I said, keeping my voice cool and level, knowing Scarlett was probably going to be a little pissed at me for what I was about to do. "I think I can take her anywhere she wants to go and claim some kind of mating bond, you jackass."

The woods stood silent, the world still as all four men stared at me, eyes wide.

"When?" Gates asked, his head cocked to the side.

I shrugged, still growling, still pissed. "A few days ago. It was the first time I'd met her."

Phoenix jerked at that, and I could practically see him putting the pieces together. We'd been at his house, in his living room, and I'd not told him what happened when Scarlett walked in. He had to remember her saying "no" and running for the door.

"Why didn't you say anything?" Rebel asked.

I shrugged. "She's private, and it hasn't been the easiest start for us. I didn't want her to have to deal with the added pressure of everyone knowing about this."

"I...I'm sorry. I didn't know she was your mate." Phoenix shook his head, but then his eyes widened. "She ran away that day, though."

"She came back," I said, simple words for a not so simple couple of days.

"I wish I would have known," Phoenix said.

"Now you do." I kept my eyes hard as I gave him a look that I hoped made him aware of how seriously I was taking this. "I'll never hurt her."

Gates gave me a one-armed hug, slapping my back in the process and making me flinch. And by the smirk on his face, he'd hit those burns on purpose. The jackass. "Congratulations. Welcome to the club. Be prepared for your space to be invaded by all things glittery."

"Charlotte hates glitter." Rebel smiled and replaced Gates, whispering his own congratulations as he smacked my shoulder. Phoenix followed, apologizing, reminding me that Scarlett was a package deal and he was part of that package. I just nodded, ready to hunt, ready to move on with this mission. If it were my mate out there, I'd want everyone focused and on point. And that was exactly how I intended to act—as if it were my mate in danger. It was a sign of respect for my mated brethren.

"So, we ready to hunt now that the coffee klatch is closed?" Jameson asked. His voice was filled with irritation, but his expression when he met my eyes was anything but. Loneliness, jealousy, and impatience. It rolled off him in waves. Seeping out of him. A man possessed by loss.

"Yeah, man," I said, letting him keep his secret for as long as he needed to. "Let's run."

DEEP IN THE WOODS, as the sky shifted from pitch black to the gray of almost dawn, we slipped through the trees toward the pack camp. Four of us had watched for hours, even circling around the site to verify buildings and terrain. We saw no movement, no shifters, no sign of Kalie, though the forest reeked of shifters. So we'd gone back to the motel to grab our secret weapon—her mate.

Gideon led our group through the darkness, his gray coat barely visible in the night. The new moon hung in the starry black above, reflecting little light to the forest floor. Packs took advantage of nights like these when the moon sat dark and waiting. They would race through the night, playing in their animal forms, jumping and running and fucking in the deeper shadows. But there would be no playing tonight, not for our group. We stalked carefully, on full alert, waiting and watching to determine our best course of action to find Omega Kalie. To save her.

The Cleaners had arrived while we'd been scouting the pack property, led by Bez who'd worked with Gates during Kaija's kidnapping. He'd been deeply involved in the missing Omega cases from the start, handling the more violent aspects of interrogation. I'd worked with him before and respected him, so that made their presence and direction easy to take.

The Cleaners were working their way in from the opposite direction, coordinating with our movements to trap the pack members in one big net.

Unfortunately, there were no pack members in the camp to trap.

Gideon paused by a tree overlooking the camp, head up, ears perked, listening and sniffing for any sign of Kalie. Body stiff, completely focused, ready for war. The camp sat less than a hundred yards away, close enough that he should be able to feel her, smell her, pinpoint her location even through the drugs. And yet he stood still as a statue, unsure. Lost.

I was beginning to lose hope, starting to plan how to track these bastards down in my head, when a car approached. The engine rumbled through the trees, growing louder as it neared.

A nondescript older model sedan appeared from the driveway leading to the dirt road on the north side of the property. The Cleaners' side. With little more than a quiet huff from Jameson, we enacted our plan. Creeping under the brush, spreading out, hiding ourselves among the twigs and dirt. Forming a V-shape pointing away from the camp with Jameson and Rebel at the nearest ends and myself at the rear. The fastest of us all and, therefore, the last line of defense.

The car doors opened almost at once, and four shifters scuttled out. A tall man with brown hair and tattoos covering his arms pulled a woman behind him. Average height, exceptionally skinny and pale, she stumbled as he dragged her toward a cabin, her red hair hanging flat and dull past her shoulders. Kalie.

Gideon growled and inched forward, his eyes locked on his mate. Jameson turned and snapped his jaws, warning him to stay put, to stay back. To wait. My tail twitched, my wolf ready to battle, my inner cat ready to hunt. The two had very different styles, but tonight they were both on board for some tracking and fighting. We had a ton of frustration to burn off, and the fuckers dragging that poor woman across the dirt would be the ones who suffered under our jaws.

"Get her inside," one of the men said, his voice carrying across the quiet forest.

"What's the plan?" Tattoo asked, spinning to face his packmate, knocking Kalie off her feet. Gideon inched closer, growling low but consistent.

"We wait to see if the drugs take effect. If they do, Aaric breeds her. If they don't, we cull her as a dud." The man spat and ran his hand over his face. "You hear me, bitch? You've got twenty-four hours to go into heat. After that, it's over. I'm not dragging your worthless ass around anymore."

Tattoo shoved Kalie into a cabin and slammed the door, stomping toward the car. Gideon's growl grew louder, stronger. Every wolf in our group responded in kind, quiet but not quiet enough. Instinctual, uncontrollable. These fuckers had obviously harmed Gideon's mate. If that were Scarlett, I'd have already attacked.

"When will Aaric be back?" Another shifter asked, this one short and thin. Scrawny almost. A human turned shifter, or Anbizen, was my guess. And a recent one at that. He moved like a human, not enough wolf in his steps to have been changed for long. A kid who'd soon be regretting his decision to join this particular group.

"In a few hours. He had a meeting with The King and didn't expect to be released until dawn."

"So what do we do until—"

A single twig breaking behind me was the only warning I had before the weight of a wolf slammed into my back, the burn of teeth in my neck making me snarl. I jumped and rolled, trying to dislodge the beast, but he held tight. It took some serious twisting to get my claws on his side, near his belly, almost close enough to cut him open. He released his hold on me, his wolf instincts to protect such a delicate area giving me a moment of reprieve.

The dark wolf stood, snarling, my blood dripping from his jaws. I circled him, letting my wolf use his instincts for this fight. My tiger stood in his hunting stance, ready to pounce if needed, wanting to use his claws as well.

Ignoring the battle erupting around me, I kept my head high, challenging the fucker who'd snuck up on me, waiting him out. Planning his death.

He lunged low, going for my legs with a snarl...a rookie mistake. I jumped and raced around, aiming for his back leg, reaching, snarling, clamping my teeth on him.

The weight of a second wolf on my back knocked me off my trajectory and forced me to miss, rolling me into the dirt. The sneaky fucker gripped me by the ruff of my neck, hanging on as I twisted and snapped. Bastard was just out of my reach, and two of his friends were circling closer. Waiting their turn. Watching for the first sign of weakness from me. My tiger surged forward, ready to jump into the action, but I held him back. There were too many other shifters around, too many of my teammates who couldn't know my truth.

My hesitation to reveal myself was the opportunity my attackers had been waiting for. The two wolves jumped, one slicing his claws across my hip and the other clamping down on my shoulder. I felt the tiger rush to take control, slid into the tingles of a shift to another form, but it was too late. Far too late.

Another bite, a vicious pull, and the tear of the flesh across my shoulders before the weight of more wolves piled on top of me. Crushing me into the dirt.

EIGHTEEN

Scarlett

SIX DAYS. IT HAD been six days since Shadow left for North Dakota with the rest of the team. Six days of worry, waiting, and silence. The last message I'd received had said they were getting close to the state line and he wouldn't be able to talk or text until the mission was over.

Six days of nothing since then. And not just for me.

The tension in the denhouse—the place the mates of Feral Breed members had basically taken ownership of as we waited to hear anything from our men—increased as every sunset lit up the front windows without a single phone call. Without a chime or a ping.

We spent our days huddled together at the tables in the bar area, cell phones out with the ringtones turned all the way up, trying to distract each other with small talk and plans for the carnival. I had no idea what the others were doing at night, after we finally surrendered to the need to go home. If they were anything like me, they were pacing, crying, punching pillows, eating ice cream, and obsessively checking their phones. Maybe they were all hanging out together, sharing the weight of their nerves among themselves. If they were, I hadn't been invited.

Not that any of them knew Shadow was my mate. Not that I had the guts to tell them. Not even my sister, Zuri, knew the truth. Not yet. She had so much on her plate with the new house, a wedding, and a baby on the way. Plus Phoenix was with Shadow, making her just as worried as I was. She didn't need more stress.

Thank the Goddess, though, that Amber knew. She ate the ice cream with me and held me when the stress got to be too much, when I curled up on the couch and cried. She also sat at the denhouse day after day with me, waiting for word, distracting all of us with her organizational skills as she set us to tasks ranging from phone calls to carnival ride research.

Six days had never seemed like such a lifetime.

"Hey, sis." Zuri pulled a barstool over and placed her phone on the bar right next to mine. Both dark and silent. Stupid useless devices.

"What's up, momma?" I asked, pasting a weak smile on my face. "How's my favorite niece treating you?"

Zuri shook her head, snorting a laugh. "She's your only niece."

"Favorite by default is still favorite."

"What are you going to do if it's a boy?"

I rolled my eyes, hard. "You're a Weaver, an elemental witch from a long line of elemental witches. You're not having a boy."

"The wolf genes may override ours. We don't know enough to have any idea of what's going on with the baby." Zuri placed her hands on her belly, her face drawn and a frown forming as she looked down at the bump. "Shit, what if it's a boy?"

The thought made my heart jump. A male Weaver? Witches weren't men, ever. And the thought of Zuri's baby not having some kind of magick inside didn't sit right with me. No way. That baby would be a witch like the rest of us; no wolfy genes could dominate our innate power.

Seeing the weight of Zuri's worries wearing her down, I

placed my hand over hers, raising my eyebrows and catching her eye.

"If it's a boy, then you'd better learn as much as you can about the peen. Get up close and personal with Phoenix; I'm sure he won't mind." I pursed my lips. "Damn, if it's a boy, I'm going to have to learn how to dye all those pretty pink things I bought. Gray. Gray might work. Or black. You won't mind if I make your son look goth, will you?"

She snorted. "Funny."

"I try." I edged closer and lowered my voice. "So are you going to have an ultrasound to find out?"

She sighed and nodded. "As soon as the guys get back. Shadow was supposed to take care of it, since we can't really deal with a regular doctor. I guess if the baby is part wolf, they can actually show signs of their wolf side in the womb or be wolf-born."

I sat back, widening my eyes. "You mean not only is there a chance that you have an actual penis growing in your belly, it could be a dog penis?"

Zuri snorted a laugh and smacked my arm. "First off, wolf, not dog as Phoenix just loves to remind me. Second, said penis would be in my uterus, not my belly. And third, quit talking about my possible son's penis. You're freaking me out."

"Oh no, this is too good. Until you know the sex of the baby, I'm running with the whole 'there's a penis inside you' all the time. So you better get on that ultrasound planning."

She blinked and took a deep breath before pasting on the fakest smile I'd ever seen her wear. "When Shadow and Phoenix come home, we'll get it done."

And by the Goddess did those words make my stomach sink to the floor. When…not if. When Shadow comes home. I glanced at the phones, willing one to light, to ring. But they lay dark and silent as ever, disappointing me as they'd been doing for six solid days.

Sighing, I reached out and grabbed her hand, the words about Shadow and me trying so hard to come out. She deserved to know, to celebrate with me, but this was not a time for celebration. This was a time for worry…for fear. For clinging to hope with both hands and refusing to give up.

"They'll be back soon," I said, the words soft, the conviction I'd had even two days ago fading.

"Yeah," she whispered, looking no more sure of their return than I felt.

Charlotte and Kaija joined us a few minutes later, the two looking as horrible as Zuri, as badly as I felt. But at least they could all commiserate together. I stood on the outside, not because of their doing, but because of my own. Only Amber knew how hard I was taking the radio silence from the guys. She knew how desperately I wanted to hear from Shadow, had watched me pace and worry for hours on end. She also knew that I couldn't stand to sleep in my own bed anymore. I'd been staying in Shadow's apartment each night, jumping at every sound, wishing for the slide of a key in a lock. Wearing his shirts and curling my body around his pillow.

"I need ice cream," Zuri said, breaking the heavy silence that had descended upon us.

"Oh, that sounds good." Calla walked over, smiling her greetings as she joined our sad little party. "I still crave dairy products all the time. I blame the breastfeeding."

"And on that note, I need tequila," Charlotte added, standing up and heading behind the bar. "Ladies, it's been a rough week. I say we get sloshed."

"I'm in," I called.

Zuri shook her head and pointed at her growing belly. "Uh, duh."

Charlotte rolled her eyes. "I don't just mix cocktails, Miss Azurine. I can also make one hell of a mean milk shake."

"Sounds perfect." Zuri grinned, a real smile this time

though she still looked tired and worn.

"Oh, what the hell," Calla said. "I've got enough breast milk in the freezer to feed Aliyana for a month. Hook me up with a spiked milk shake."

"Remind me never to go digging in your freezer." I winked at Calla as she flushed red before pointing at Zuri.

"Ali's asleep in Rebel's office. Can you be my backup parent since Beast is working at the shop?" Calla asked.

Zuri grinned. "Gimme the monitor. I could use some baby snuggles today. And remind me to tell you about Phoenix and the baby carrier next time you're at my house."

"Oh gosh, yeah. I die every time Beast straps Ali to his chest." Calla handed Zuri a plastic, walkie-talkie type device. "But remind me to tell you what happens when your milk lets down during sex."

I felt my face scrunch as I took two steps back. "I don't think I want to know what that means."

"What, sex?" Calla asked, smirking, giving me a very Beast-like eyebrow raise. "Well, you see, young Scarlett, when a man and a woman—"

"Or a woman and a woman," Zuri said, smirking.

Kaija shrugged. "Or a man and a man."

Zuri rolled her eyes. "Look, when two—" she waved off Charlotte, who looked ready to interrupt again "—or three or four or any number of people really like one another—"

I huffed and gave her a playful shoulder nudge. "I know what sex means, you trollop."

"Trollop?" Charlotte said with a laugh while handing Kaija and me shots. "Who uses that word anymore?"

"My sister," Amber said as she walked into the bar. "Though why, I have no idea."

I shrugged. "Better than the alternatives."

Amber rolled her eyes and wrapped an arm around my shoulder. "How're you doing?"

I glanced at the other women, but they were all ignoring us, laughing and talking as Charlotte started liquoring most of them up. "So far, so good."

"Liar." She watched me, her eyes unfocused, wearing her Magic Eight Ball look. "You'll be okay."

"I'm more worried about Shadow," I whispered. "I can feel him, but it's so faint. I don't understand this mating link thing."

"Hey, Amber," Charlotte hollered, interrupting us. "You want a shot?"

Amber gave me a small smile and an arm squeeze before turning toward the busty blonde. "Why the hell not?"

Six shots and a bartop sing-along to "I Touch Myself" later, I lifted my head off my folded arms enough to peer blurrily at Charlotte. "What's vibrating?"

"Trollop," Calla yelled, giggling drunkenly.

Charlotte shook her head slowly, staring drunkenly at a slice of lime in her glass. "Don't look at me."

"No, really, I hear it too." Zuri jumped up and hurried toward the bar, rubbing her sternum. "By the Goddess, this heartburn is killing me."

Calla looked around the bar, her eyes bleary. "Where's Kaija?"

"She and Amber went home after the fourth shot," Charlotte said. "It's getting louder."

The three of us quieted down, silent and listening, glancing worriedly at the phones lined up side by side like normal. The silent, dark phones.

"What is that noise?" I asked, the rumble growing louder.

"Yo, crazy ladies," a shifter who'd been introduced to me as Numbers yelled from across the room. "Your boys are back."

It took exactly two seconds for his words to navigate their way through my drunken haze. It took less than that to be on my feet and running toward the back door where the blessed sound of motorcycles pulling onto the lot reached my ears. The rest of the girls followed me, all of us stopping just outside—right next to a practically vibrating Kaija—while the men we prayed were our mates rolled to a stop.

"You could have told us," Charlotte hissed at Kaija.

She smirked and shook her head. "Once I felt him so close, I couldn't wait anymore. My bond was too loud. The benefit of being a shifter mated to a shifter, I guess."

As each man dismounted his bike, his mate raced across the asphalt for him. First Charlotte, then Zuri, then Kaija. I stood and waited, wringing my hands so hard I thought I would break one, watching for Shadow, wondering if the fourth bike finally pulling onto the lot would be his. Feeling the pull of the mating bond but not clearly enough to know for sure.

The man barely had his helmet off before I was racing across the asphalt, passing the others by, completely oblivious to anything other than the long, dark hair falling over black leather.

"Oh, blessed be," I cried.

"Hey, Firecracker." Shadow smiled and caught me when I threw myself into his arms. I tucked my face into his neck as the tears broke through, letting down my guard now that I knew he was back. That he was safe.

"You didn't call," I whispered. "None of you called."

"I know, and I'm sorry. I knew you'd be worried, but there was nothing any of us could do. Jameson put us on radio silence as soon as we got to North Dakota. That order was reinforced by Blaze since we had to spend a few days in Chicago with the team to go over every detail of the job and heal up."

A shiver flew down my spine at the thought of why they'd need to "heal up" as he so casually said. But he was back, walking, talking, and holding me. Whatever had happened couldn't have been too bad…at least I hoped.

I peered up at him, so very thankful just to see his gray eyes again. "It didn't go well?"

He shrugged, the motion making him wince, making my heart jump. "It went well enough. We accomplished our main goal."

"But?"

"Yo, Shadow." Rebel sauntered over, a tear-streaked Charlotte tucked under his arm. "How about we take care of your bandages before I head home with my lady."

"Bandages?" I asked, that flinch from a moment ago replaying in my head. My blood turned to ice in my veins, fear almost stealing my voice. "Why do you need bandages?"

Shadow glared at Rebel. "It's not a big deal."

I crossed my arms over my chest. "Shadow."

"Scarlett." He pulled me closer, untangling my arms from where I'd crossed them to wrap them around his waist. Breathing me in as he nuzzled into my neck. "I'm okay."

Reluctantly, I pulled away, pushing on his chest and forcing a little space between us. Refusing to be distracted by his naughty lips on my skin. When he didn't offer up any details, I turned to Rebel. "What happened?"

Rebel smirked and looked me over, cocky as ever. Charlotte appeared confused by the way Shadow and I were wrapped around one another, not that I blamed her. Still, there were more important things to deal with than satisfying her curiosity. Like a mate who refused to tell me why he needed bandages.

"I swear to the Goddess, if someone doesn't start talking—"

"Fuckers snuck up on us." Phoenix walked over, smiling at me the same way as Rebel had. "Wouldn't have been a big deal since taking out that pack didn't take too long, but one big sucker bit a chunk out of Shadow before he knew what hit him. Took three of us to knock him off."

"Yeah, after he had his teeth in me." Shadow leaned down and ran his cheek over the top of my head. "I think my own guys did more damage than the enemy. They almost skinned me."

I melted against him, running my hands over his back carefully, not sure where I could and couldn't touch but needing contact. Craving skin. "Like friendly fire, but with teeth. A little friendly biting?"

Shadow growled, low and quiet against my ear as he whispered, "Is that an offer?"

"Okay, what the hell is this?" Zuri asked.

I lifted my head, staying in Shadow's arms as she stared at the two of us. "What?"

"This," she spat, her face a mask of rage, wagging her finger at Shadow. "You're going to play my sister like this?"

"Zuri," Phoenix said, grabbing her arm.

"No." Zuri shook him off and continued her attack on Shadow as I bit back a smile. My sister on a protective rant was a remarkable sight, especially with her pregnant belly in the way. "You think you can just lead her on? Fuck around with her until the real thing shows up? What happens when you find your fated mate, huh? What do you intend to do then?"

Shadow stayed calm, his face almost expressionless as he said, "I intend to settle down and rock my mate's world with lots and lots of sex every single day."

He shrugged and smirked when I met his gaze, so I gave him a nod. Yup, sounded good to me.

Zuri, though, still looked angry, her cheeks turning red as she yelled, "And what about Scarlett? What's going to happen to her while you're off having all this sex with your mate?"

Shadow grinned, wicked and wide. "If I know your sister like I think I do, I'm pretty sure she'll enjoy the sex."

I narrowed my eyes as the guys who'd ridden in with Shadow chuckled, hiding their grins as best they could. "You told them, didn't you?"

"I had to." He shrugged and gave me a wink. "Hard to hide burn marks when you have to get naked in front of other people. It's not like those handprints could have been anything else."

"Oh." My neck flushed warm, my ears burning. Hadn't thought about that aspect of his being a wolf shifter before. Though at least they'd been on his back and not someplace more...telling.

"Oh?" Zuri asked, still looking angry and confused. "What 'oh'?"

I shrugged and smiled at my sister, tossing her own words from only a few months ago back at her. "He's kind of mine."

She opened and closed her mouth, speechless. But then she snapped her jaws shut with a click. "What do you mean, kind of?"

"Sort of." I shrugged.

"Sort of?" She crossed her arms over her chest, glaring at me.

I nodded, biting back a grin. "Mostly."

Zuri huffed. "Is he or is he not your red thread?"

I looked up at Shadow, smiling, basking in his return grin. "Yeah, I guess he is."

"Oh." Her anger dissolved, her face pulling up in a grin. "Well, that's so much better than you two just humping like bunnies and waiting for the ax to fall. Okay." But then... "Hey, why didn't you tell me, you brat?"

"C'mon, Zuri," Phoenix said, pulling her toward the denhouse. "Leave the two lovebirds alone. It's time to go home."

"She could have told me," Zuri said, voice loud and a little harsh. But as much as I loved my sister, as much as I wanted to apologize and give her every gory detail of the last couple of weeks, I had no attention to spare. Shadow practically consumed me, the heat in his eyes drawing out my own, making me burn for him. Making me needy for his touch.

"You're kind of mine," I whispered, biting back my smile.

He shrugged, playing casual even as the look in his eyes intensified, pulling me closer. "If you want me to be."

"I'd like that," I replied, sliding my hands under his jacket. "As long as that means I get to be yours."

He gave me a mock frown. "Just don't try to boss me around."

"Wouldn't think of it. Now kiss me." I yanked on his shirt, pulling him down to my level.

"See? Already so bossy."

I pulled back as he moved to kiss me, denying him. Teasing him. "Well, if you'd prefer that I sit all meek and quiet…"

Shadow squeezed me tightly as he growled. "Woman, I swear to your Goddess, if you don't give me those lips right now—"

He never finished his sentence. I rose up onto the balls of my feet and pressed my mouth to his, running my tongue along the seam of his lips until he opened. Until he kissed me roughly, with teeth and tongue and heavy breaths. He wrapped his arms around me and pulled me off my feet. Holding me, giving me what I'd been missing for days. His touch, his taste, his scent. Him. I wrapped my arms around his neck, squeezing, sliding my hands down his back.

Until he hissed and set me down.

"Sorry," he said, reaching to rub his shoulder, making my fingers itch with the need to touch and heal him. To do something.

"No, that was my fault," I said, holding on to his wrist to keep my connection to him. "I got a little carried away."

He grinned. "I like it when I get to carry you away. Reminds me of a night not so long ago."

I snorted and shook my head. "Such a charming mouth."

Shadow shrugged, pulling me closer, running his nose along my cheek as I giggled. "I don't remember you complaining about my mouth."

"C'mon, Romeo," Rebel said, interrupting us. "Let's get those bandages changed, and then you can go charm your new mate."

Shadow sighed and nodded at his den president, but his eyes stayed locked on mine. Wary again. Worried.

"Wait for me?"

My heart flared, burning around the edges as the guilt over what I'd done to hurt him circled around. It was my fault he looked so nervous, my fault he worried that I wouldn't wait for him. That I didn't want him. I needed to convince him that this was it...*he* was it. Instead of giving him a big, dramatic sigh and saying something sarcastic like "If I must" as I'd normally do, I used his actions against him.

I stared him right in the eye, open and honest as I said a simple but firm, "Yes."

He froze, peering at me, a slow smile spreading across his lips. "I like that answer. I'd like to hear it a lot more often."

I curled into his side and slid a hand under his shirt, needing one more moment of skin-on-skin contact. "So bossy."

He shrugged. "You like it."

"Yeah," I said as we strolled inside. "I guess I do."

"Scarlett," Rebel said from just outside his office door, flanked by Kaija and Gates. "Why don't you and Charlotte wait for us in the bar?"

Shadow stiffened, muscles going tight under my fingers. I pressed my hand against the small of his back, reassuring him, reassuring myself as well.

"I think I'd rather stay close," I said. Rebel glanced at Shadow, questioning, a look of warning though I had no idea why.

"It...you might want to stay outside." Shadow's quiet, stumbling voice made my stomach drop. Made me want to grab him and run. Made my hands and body heat as my fire stoked within.

"Why would I want to stay outside?"

"Scarlett," Shadow said, pulling me to the side and

crowding me against the wall. "The tears are big and they're not healing as fast as they should. It's been a long ride. I have no idea what shape my back's in right now." He leaned closer, forehead against mine, eyes worn and drawn. "I don't want you to see this, or to worry."

I bit my lip, holding back the burn in my eyes, as I nodded. "As if I haven't been worried about you every moment for the past six days?"

"I know, and I'm sorry." He kissed my nose before taking a step back, resigned to keeping me out. "Just wait here. It'll only be a few minutes."

As he walked into Rebel's office, the big metal door closing behind him, I slid down the wall to the floor. I hated these secrets, hated that he couldn't tell me what had happened or why they'd been in North Dakota in the first place. But I cared for him more than I hated the secrets, so I sat in the hall. And I waited. Charlotte joined me, holding out a hand. Giving me something to cling to. And I did… Desperately.

"He'll be fine," she said, not sounding any more confident than I felt.

"He's the doctor," I said. "He's the one with the training, but he can't treat himself."

"Yeah, but Rebel's handy with that stuff. He'll take care of your boy." She shifted closer, bumping her shoulder against mine. "A few minutes, and Shadow will have clean bandages and—"

She never finished her sentence. Shadow's growl rumbled through the door, loud and deep and menacing. Pained. I closed my eyes, trying not to imagine why he had to be growling, but it was no use. I knew he was hurting…felt it.

"You should probably let go of me," I said, biting back my words, barely controlling my temper as his growl turned to a soft whimper. The rush of heat building within made my bones hurt and my skin tighten…made me fear for Charlotte's safety.

"Why?" Charlotte asked, though she did release my hand.

"Because things are about to get a little warm."

For five minutes, I sat on the floor of the hallway with my head down, my hair glowing, and sparks falling from my palms as I listened to Shadow be rebandaged. Even the air moved in the hall, a little extra magick coming to join the party of my out-of-control emotions. Five minutes as Shadow growled and groaned, snapped and yipped. Five minutes longer than I should have sat out there.

When he whimpered a second time, I jumped up and flew toward the door. Fuck staying in the hall, my red thread needed me. I could feel it, could practically sense his pain.

Rebel, Gates, and Kaija jumped when I stormed into the office, all three of them looking at me with wide eyes. Shadow lay across Rebel's desk, chest down, back up, clinging to the edges to that point that his knuckles were pure white.

"Scarlett, baby," he called, his voice rough. "I'm okay."

But he was definitely not okay. Not at all.

"Get out." My voice came out like a hiss, like a curse. Every inch of me hurt, ached with the fire running through my veins, but I couldn't stop it. Couldn't extinguish the blaze. My element was strong and ready, my magick growing. I would protect my red thread no matter what, even against those he trusted.

"Scarlett," Rebel started, but I didn't let him finish. He held what I had to assume were the old bandages in his hands, stained red with blood. Shadow's blood. The entire room glowed red as I brought my hand up, twisting my fingers and setting them on fire. Orange and yellow light dancing through my skin.

"I said, get out. You've hurt him enough."

"Reb," Shadow said, his voice weak. "Just go. We'll be fine."

Rebel glanced from Shadow to me and back before he gave a single head nod. "He's cleaned up but needs new bandages to keep the area clean. Supplies are on the table there. If you need us—"

"I won't."

Kaija smirked at me as she followed the two men through the door. "Be gentle, Sparky. He's not ready for a woman like you."

I caught her eye as she winked, giving her a single nod of my head. She was right—he wasn't ready for anything but care and comfort. Something I'd never really done before, but was willing to work at for him.

As soon as they were gone, I slammed the door, shutting myself in with my mate. My very injured mate.

"What did they do to you?" My whisper came out bathed in pain, caused by the sight of his back. I quickly put out the fire on my hands so I could move closer. "By the Goddess, why?"

My handprints stood out on his skin, deep red and only slightly textured. But what screamed pain and violence, what made my tears fall and my breath catch, were the rips. All the way across his back, up one side of his shoulder, across the expanse again. Thick, reddish-purple lines stitched together. Obviously painful. Obviously healing.

And yet.

"What did they do to you?" I asked again as I placed my fingers against him, being careful to touch what little undamaged skin there was. Bite marks, smaller tears, scrapes—a myriad of marks, all marring his back. All making me want to weep.

"Friendly biting," he whispered, huffing a laugh that wasn't at all funny. "The guy wouldn't let go, so they had to knock him off me...while his teeth were still embedded in my flesh."

My fingertip brushed over a single, purple puncture wound. "Oh, Shadow."

"It's okay, Firecracker." He reached out and grabbed my hand, pulling me closer. "We had a successful mission, for the most part, just a few loose ends hanging out there. As for these marks, shifters heal fast. It's my fault I'm not already good as new."

"Your fault?"

He gave me that look, that Shadow look, that honest gaze. "Because I refused to let them cut away the skin. I would have healed faster, but I didn't want to lose your handprints."

I choked on a sob, eyes burning. "Well, shit, Shadow."

He smiled, small but bright. "I earned those burns."

I nodded and wiped my eyes, focusing on the task at hand. "Yeah, you did. And I'll make sure you keep them."

I rubbed my hands together as I began a chant I'd known most of my life, one of air and water, of the Mother Goddess and the power of the earth, one of healing. Shadow lay still, watching me, trusting me.

It'd been months since I'd used my powers like this, all the way open to the magick around me...full-out witch. I'd missed it, missed the tingle it left under my skin. So much softer than the fire that had been growing increasingly uncomfortable as I ignored my base magick.

I moved my hands over his back, not touching but close. Feeling his energy, giving him mine.

"May I ruin your shirt?" I asked, needing more, needing to do things right.

Shadow paused but then nodded. "Sure."

I grabbed the black fabric from the couch, lighting a single fingertip on fire to burn an edge before ripping it up the front. Laying it across his back, I covered the tears in his flesh, made a circle with the fabric. Complete and unbroken. A binding loop.

"I do not bind the body or the spirit of this man," I whispered, moving my hands over the circle of black, pushing all my magick and power through them and into Shadow. "I bind the disease residing in the flesh, that it may enter this circle. That it may reside within so only flames can release it hence."

Three times I chanted the spell, keeping my hands close,

giving Shadow my full attention. When I finished, I lifted the black fabric, holding it up and facing all four corners to show my love and respect for the elements.

"Goddess of the earth, of light and love, thank you for your healing. I offer this binding to the element of fire, that only flames can release the negativity within to begin a process of renewal."

Clutching the fabric, I allowed my fire to burn through my palms. The black strips burst into flames, disappearing into a smoky, ashy pile of dust in a matter of seconds.

"So mote it be."

The air, charged with magick, brushed over my skin. A gentle caress. A welcome back. I'd missed doing spells, but the pain of our banishment from the coven had kept me from practicing. I'd lost so much when we left, but I'd gained more, found my balance. Found my future once I met Shadow.

My inner fire receded, calming and cooling, no longer painful. Magick balancing magick, as it should be.

"I've never seen you do something like that before."

I turned, smiling at Shadow. He'd sat up, leaning a hip against the edge of the desk, shirtless and smiling and beautiful.

"It's been a while," I said with a shrug. He held out a hand, beckoning me. I answered him with an eagerness I couldn't contain. Rushing to him, curling into his hold. "I missed you."

"I missed you too, Firecracker." He nuzzled into my neck, his favorite spot it seemed, and placed small kisses to the skin there. "I can't imagine what I would do if…"

I ran a hand over his arm, wanting his words, wanting him. "If what?"

He swallowed hard, clinging to me. "If it were you. If they'd taken you."

My heart cracked, paused, the fear in his voice making me ache for him. And whoever was living the nightmare in his thoughts.

"It wasn't me. I'm right here." I rubbed my hand over his hair, soothing him as much as I could with my touch.

"Scarlett?"

"Shadow?"

"I'd never give up." The intensity in his voice had me pulling back, staring down at him in question. "If someone took you away from me, I'd never give up searching. I'd find you, no matter what. I want you to know that."

I nodded, confused and heartbroken. Whatever happened in North Dakota had harmed him in more than just the physical. The way he spoke, the words, the feel of his hands shaking as he gripped my hips. Something had scared him.

"I know," I all but cooed. "I'd find you, too."

NINETEEN

Shadow

MY HEART BEAT FAST as I hopped up the porch stairs at Scarlett's house, a sure sign of my nerves. Not that I had much reason to be nervous. We'd been sleeping in the same bed since I came home from North Dakota. Three days of lying beside her, holding her, kissing her, but not much else. She called it taking things slow so I could heal; I called it my absolute favorite kind of torture. But tonight was different…we were going out on our first official date.

First and possibly last…at least for a few weeks. I'd told Scarlett about the "loose ends" Jameson and I still needed to deal with back in Chicago. Those loose ends included a missing pack Alpha and Beta from the group that'd taken Kalie, a lack of leads on who the hell The King really was, and a complete information dead end. For being a successful mission—we'd decimated the pack, saved the girl, reunited her with her mate, and gotten them both safely to Merriweather Fields for medical care—we'd failed. Miserably.

Jameson was just waiting for me to participate in the charity ride, then we were heading out to bang on doors and rattle cages.

"Young Shadow," Amber said when she opened the door, a sarcastic smile on her face. "What can I do for you this evening?"

Shaking off the negative thoughts about my job, I bent into a mock bow, playing along. "I'm here for Miss Scarlett."

"Well, come on in." She stepped back and beckoned me inside. I gave her a smile as I passed, too busy looking for my mate to pay her a lot of attention. "Scarlett will be down in a second."

"Okay, thanks," I said, glancing her way before training my eyes on the stairs again. Anxious. Ready.

Before Scarlett could appear, Amber made a choking sound, causing me to turn. Her eyes were wide, pupils blown as if under the influence of some kind of drug. But worse than that was the fact that while she was looking at me, her eyes were so unfocused, it appeared as if she was looking through me. Seeing things I couldn't. An act that made my blood run cold.

"Are you okay?" I asked, steeling myself for whatever she might throw at me.

"Your fight can't be won without loss," she hissed, her head cocked to the side and her hair lifting in a breeze I sensed but couldn't feel.

"Excuse me?" I took a step back, willing Scarlett to come down the stairs, not comfortable around Amber's brand of magick.

"He lifted the shadows in a time of need, but his time is up." She closed her eyes for a moment, a sad smile forming on her lips. "Another avoided it once and wears the stain, but they've always been meant to fall. The smoke will call them."

The growl that rumbled through me was unstoppable and dark, the burn of fear flaring bright under my skin. "You want to explain what you mean and who you're talking about?"

"She probably doesn't even know." Scarlett appeared at my side, smelling like heaven and sin all at once, staring down her sister. "Her visions are acting up."

She reached for Amber, holding on to her arms as the two took a moment to breathe together. To settle one another. To whisper quiet words of calm and comfort. After a few minutes, Amber closed her eyes again and dropped her chin to her chest, her entire body sagging as if exhausted.

"Without a grounding point, sometimes things get away from me," Amber said, her voice quiet. "I'm sorry if I scared you."

I gave her a small smile when she glanced up, relieved that her eyes were now bright and focused.

"Better?" Scarlett asked, only smiling once her sister nodded. Still, she paused, uncertain. "Do you need me to stay?"

"No," Amber replied, shooing us toward the door. "Go out. I'm fine."

Scarlett still waited, obviously uncertain. "Okay then. My bag's already in the trunk. I won't be back tonight, but I'll be at the denhouse in the morning for the ride to Chicago. You're picking up the other girls there too, right?"

"Yeah. We're all taking one car since the rest of you will probably ride back with your guys." Amber nodded, looking exhausted. The two women exchanged a long hug before pulling apart.

"You sure you're okay?" Scarlett asked.

Amber huffed. "Yeah, yeah, go on, have fun, do things I wouldn't." She grinned before her eyes went unfocused again, just a flash, something I doubted Scarlett even noticed. "Stay off the carousel."

"What carousel?" Scarlett asked, her words slow, her face filled with concern.

"No idea. The smoke is blocking everything." Amber rubbed her temple. "Just...don't go near one."

Scarlett watched her sister amble toward the back of the house before turning toward me. She seemed distracted, concerned, not that I blamed her. Whatever was going on with

Amber had made quite the impression on me. A bad impression.

"Would you rather stay home?" I asked, wishing she'd say no but understanding she may need to.

"No, she'll call me if she needs me." Scarlett huffed as we walked out the front door. "I've got to talk to Phoenix about her."

"Why Phoenix?"

"He's supposed to be able to help her, some kind of wolf spirit air magick balancing act." She shook her head as I held the car door open for her, pasting on a bright smile I knew she didn't mean. "No more bad stuff. Where are we going?"

"We can cancel," I said, staring into her green eyes, pulling her against me. "I can hang out with you here so we can keep an eye on your sister."

Scarlett's smile brightened, turning true. Making my heart soar. "You are the sweetest, but that's not necessary. She'll be okay for the night, and then tomorrow we'll go to Chicago. A change of scenery may do her good."

I leaned down, placing a soft kiss on her pink lips. "If you're sure."

"I'm sure," she mumbled before deepening the kiss. Our mouths moved in concert, tongues sliding together as if we'd done this a million times. And maybe we had. We'd been taking it slow these last few nights but hadn't stopped exploring one another. Torture…pure, blissful torture.

When she finally pulled back, she gave me a saucy smile. "So, where are we going?"

"Dinner, and then dancing." I helped her into the car and shut her door before hurrying around to my side.

"*Where* are we going for dinner?" she asked as I slid into the driver's seat.

"You'll see." The engine roared as I turned the key. "You look beautiful, by the way."

"You always say that." She tried to sound flippant, but she

couldn't hide the small smile my compliment brought out. Beautiful didn't begin to cover it.

I ran a finger down her cheek, and then threw the car into reverse. "You're always beautiful."

"Charmer," she said with a smirk.

"I do my best."

The restaurant was crowded, but my reservation got us seated at a table with minimal waiting. Wine, bread, and more food than was probably a good idea were all consumed while we made small talk and laughed. It was a real, honest to goodness, normal date. Something I'd never experienced, and something I found myself enjoying much more than I ever thought possible. Especially as Scarlett got a little tipsy and started telling me about growing up in a coven full of witches.

"I swear to the Goddess," Scarlett said, her face red and her eyes wide. "They've tormented me about that damn porch for years, but I was not the one who set it on fire."

I coughed to hold back my laugh. "You can see how they'd doubt that, right?"

Scarlett rolled her eyes, sitting back when the waiter came to place her dessert in front of her. Once he left us, she leaned forward again and pointed her fork at me.

"Elemental witches can control more than one element, my friend. Zuri's a water witch with a leaning toward air and the ability to join me in controlling fire. I'm a fire witch with a hefty control of earth magick and a little air teachings." She smirked, her eyes bright. "If you ever see what looks like a water tornado on fire, you can trust it's Zuri and me screwing around."

"I…okay." I laughed, not knowing what else to say. Fiery water tornado?

Scarlett waved me off. "And Amber…well, she's the air witch, the psychic. But she also has an uncanny control over fire. She can light things up that no one else can, other than me. I think she's the one who burned the porch down."

"Of course." I grinned at her, shaking my head slowly. God, she was gorgeous. Full of life and energy, of love and spark. I wanted to bask in her, let her tell me all her stories. I wanted to take her away somewhere we could be alone and hoard all her attention. I just wanted *her*.

She smiled, a little questioning in her eyes. "What are you laughing about?"

"Nothing," I said, grabbing her hand and leaning across the table. "You're beautiful."

She rolled her eyes, neck flushing, drawing my eyes down to her chest. "You always say that."

I recaptured her gaze, tugging her closer. "And I always mean it. You're beautiful...especially on the inside. So damn independent and confident. I like that about you, your strength. It's very appealing."

Scarlett's eyes went soft, and her hand clutched mine. "You're a sweet man."

"I do my best."

Scarlett looked down at her plate, a slight flush to her cheeks. "Hey, Shadow."

"Yeah?"

"I know you said we were going dancing after this but" — she looked up at me, eyes serious— "can you take me home?"

My stomach sank and I was sure my face had to portray the sudden sense of regret flooding me. How I'd screwed up so quickly, I had no idea, but I desperately wanted to fix my mistake.

Scarlett squeezed my hand harder and brought her intense stare up to meet mine.

"Take me home...to your place."

TWENTY

Scarlett

SHADOW GRIPPED MY THIGH on the drive across town. Hard and strong, he held me in place with one hand, and yet I'd never felt more free. This was my decision. Everything we'd done and not done since he returned from North Dakota— battled, scarred, and in more pain than he wanted to admit— had been my decision. He'd never pushed me, never demanded, always let me lead. He had no problem letting me decide how far or how fast anything in our relationship went. And I had decided to move the physical side of things forward. Tonight.

When we pulled into the lot behind the denhouse, I didn't hesitate. I opened the door and stepped out into the night, striding toward the entrance. Shadow followed, catching up and placing a hand at my lower back. As if I needed guidance. As if I needed his touch. Hell, by the way my hands were shaking and my heart was racing, maybe I did. Or maybe he needed mine.

By the time we reached his apartment, my breaths were coming faster, my body had overheated, and my panties were already wet. This night, this moment, had been building for weeks. Through refusals and misunderstandings, through quiet moments between us and learning how to build a relationship on a single thread. This moment was my future.

So I walked into his space with confidence and desire, without fear, and with full control of the magick within me. No more unintentional burns from me.

As soon as Shadow closed the door behind us, I spun into his hold, grabbing his face, pulling him down to me. He wrapped his strong arms around my waist and lifted me off the ground with no effort, his show of strength making me groan into our kiss. My legs found their way around his hips, one hand fisting his hair and the other splayed across his shoulder blade, pressing into the mark I'd already given him. Holding him tight. Tying him to me.

"Scarlett," he whispered, pulling back an inch.

I closed that gap, biting his bottom lip with a smirk. "Shadow."

His growl was a constant and deep rumble in the room, like the underlying bass in a song. Meant to push things, to set the pace of the dance. To keep us moving forward.

"I don't want to rush you." He kissed me again, long, lapping strokes of his tongue against mine as he massaged my ass. Damn, I loved the feel of his hands on me. Wanted them all over. Every inch.

"You're not rushing me. If anything, I'm rushing you." I dropped my head back as he nibbled his way down my neck. Nuzzling, licking, sucking, making me crazy for more. I clung to him, pulling him in tighter, secretly wishing he'd give me a hickey. Some kind of mark. An adult equivalent of a letterman's jacket or a class ring exchanged to show that connection between us. Something like the burns he wore proudly on his back.

He chuckled and gave me one last bite before pulling back again, placing his forehead against mine, looking into my eyes as if he truly saw me. "I've been ready for anything you'd be willing to give me since the moment I saw you."

My heart melted. "I'm sorry it took me so long."

He shook his head, still smiling, still with me. "I would have waited forever."

I closed my eyes, his words making me shiver. Making me tremble. "I'm glad I didn't make you."

"Hell, me too." He chuckled, pulling me closer, hugging me with everything he had. I hugged him back, still wrapped around his body. His very hard, very strong body.

"Shadow?"

"Scarlett?"

"Can we go to bed now?"

He pulled back, his brow furrowed. "I…yeah. Of course."

A knot of dread formed in my stomach as he placed my feet back on the ground. "What? What's that look?"

"Hmmm." He glanced at me, distracted. "Oh, I just realized I've never had sex in my bed."

I stared, blinked, searched for words but found only one. "What?"

"It always seemed too intimate, I guess. I just…never brought a woman into my bedroom."

"You're joking."

"No, not at all." He shrugged and looked around his apartment. "I mean, it's not like I needed to. I just used the walls, floors, tables, chairs, the couch—"

I held up a hand, stopping him. "We're seriously going to have to get rid of every piece of furniture in this place."

A sarcastic grin spread across his face. "Does that mean you want to stay here with me?"

"After we burn the couch, the tables, rip up the carpeting, and discuss any other items that may need to go up in flames" —I shrugged— "sure."

He swept me into his arms, carrying me through the apartment and into the bedroom. "I think I know someone who can help set the stuff on fire."

"They must be a cool as hell; flames are badass." I giggled as he tossed me on the bed. Smiling, he pulled his shirt and pants off without waiting for me. I loved that about him, how confident he was in his skin, how sure. Of course, his body was toned and delicious, sexy beyond reason. There was nothing for him not to be confident about.

Lying back, watching him shed his clothing, something dark and vulnerable grew in my belly. Something much like fear. But instead of running away, I ran toward him. Sought him out.

"Shadow?"

"Scarlett?"

I fingered the edge of the pillow. "Was that true?"

He paused, staring. "Was what true?"

"What you said." I huffed and looked up at him. Mentally running toward him faster and with gusto. "Have you never had sex in your bed?"

His smile was soft, his eyes bright as he crawled over me, pushing me back to lie on the mattress.

"You are the only woman I've ever had in my bed, the only one who's ever been in this room. I told you, it seemed too intimate. Too…meaningful."

"So we have meaning?" I reached up and wrapped my arms around his neck.

"We have so much meaning, Firecracker." He let his weight come to rest on me, pressing me into the mattress. "You're the first woman in my bed and in my heart. First and last."

He kissed me slowly, deeply, as he worked on stripping me of my dress. Every move careful, every touch gentle. Intimate. Showing me where I stood, how much I meant to him. How much he cared.

When I lay naked underneath him, pinned by his weight and surrounded by his warmth, I clung to him, shaking.

"You okay?" he asked, stroking my hair.

"Yeah," I whispered. "I've just never felt like this. I've never felt so much."

He gripped me tighter, pulling me up and placing me on his lap, my legs on either side of his. "Isn't it amazing?"

I nodded into his shoulder, thankful he felt the same. That he understood. "Yeah, it really is."

Our foreplay started slowly, a simple shift of my hips, a run of his teeth along my shoulder. A building of heat within me and between us. But soon, we were pushing and pulling against one another, his erection trapped between us, my pussy sliding over it, making him wet with me, making him moan. We kissed and bit and teased our way through my first orgasm, Shadow holding me up as I groaned and shook from nothing more than rubbing against him. Keeping the pressure on my clit to make it last.

When I caught my breath, my forehead against his neck, I whispered, "Do you have a condom?"

He kissed my head and reached back, grabbing an unopened box from the nightstand. The fact that the box was still sealed shut meant something in my mind. He was starting fresh with me, as I was with him. First chances, first times, and if red threads and mates and fate had anything to say about it, this would be our last first. Together.

I took the foil package from his fingers and tore it open. Sliding back, gripping his erection in one hand, I rolled the latex down his shaft, loving the way even those simple touches made him moan and bite his lip. Wanting to make him feel as good as he made me. Once covered, I crawled back onto his lap, straddling him. Rubbing against him a little more. Still wanting to tease him even though we both knew exactly where this was going.

"Hey, Shadow?" I rotated my hips, pressing down, grinding on his cock. Sliding my hands to his shoulders, to the marks I'd left him, letting the heat within me rebrand those burns.

"Hey, Scarlett?" His voice came out harsh, his hands gripping my hips harder than before. I liked it. Liked that show of roughness.

I leaned in, put my lips right against the skin of his neck and whispered, "Make me yours."

He snarled, tossing me back on the bed and sliding on top of me, inside of me. A single thrust was all it took, one shift of his hips, and it was on. No longer gentle, no longer soft or sweet, this wasn't lovemaking or any other purple prose. This was sex. Fucking. Animalistic, harsh, and amazing. He growled and snarled his way through, biting my neck more than once as I did the same. Putting my teeth in his flesh was a need, a desire I couldn't control to mark him. Own him. Claim him as mine.

Every thrust grew harder, every deep press of his hips into mine more desperate. I wrapped my legs around him, crossing my ankles against his ass, and held on tight. Grunting, sweating, sliding across the mattress as he took me higher. As he pushed me over the edge of desire. And damn was it perfect.

Until we fell off the bed.

Not that it mattered; Shadow picked me up and lifted me back onto the mattress, my ass right at the edge. He stood with a growl, pulling my legs up, straight up, then splaying them wide. Sliding back inside, going deeper than before. The angle, the depth, the blatant view he must have had as he watched himself fucking me was so filthy. Such a turn-on. I gasped and shook as he took me, one hand on my breast, the other edging down my stomach.

"Fuck, Scarlett," he groaned as my fingers found my clit.

"Great idea." I moaned and bit my lip as I teased my clit, forming a V around it with my fingers. "You should definitely fuck Scarlett."

He huffed a laugh before increasing his pace. He spread my legs wider, forcing them down, making me groan at the change in depth and the stretch in my hips.

I kept my hands busy, pinching my nipples, spreading myself to give him an even better view, teasing his cock as it slid in and out of me. I clawed and mewled at him, but he didn't stop. The bed creaked and hit the wall, but he didn't stop. I came with a scream, trying to pull my legs together and failing, and he didn't stop. He was a man on a mission, and that mission involved fucking me half to death. Thank the Goddess for his endurance and my yoga sessions.

Moving my ankles to his shoulders, he bent over me, still buried deep in my pussy. Folding me in half, finding a way to go deeper when I'd thought that impossible. To give me more when he was already giving me so much.

"Shadow," I groaned, so tired and oversensitive but still wanting more, needing it. Needing something.

"Yeah, baby?"

"I need...I need." I rocked my head back and forth, uncertain. Needing something new, something with meaning, something—

"Bite me," I whispered, a surge of heat working up my spine at the idea of his teeth in my flesh.

He groaned at my demand, folding me farther, slowly moving his body over mine even as his hips kept up a punishing rhythm.

"Are you sure?" he asked, his voice breathy. "We can't take this back. It'll join us permanently."

"I'm sure," I said, looking into his eyes, being more truthful than ever. "I want you forever. Bite me. Make me yours."

He nodded, pulling my legs off his shoulders and letting my knees hook over his bent elbows. The shallower depth of his thrusts didn't change how good he felt inside me, how right I knew this was as he filled me again and again. He bent more, pushing me up the mattress, climbing on top of me. Thrusting hard. Keeping me on the edge of something.

He skimmed his nose along my neck. I shuddered.

He circled his tongue around a spot right where my neck met my shoulder. I groaned.

Finally, with whispered words of sweetness and devotion, he bit me. The orgasm that ripped through my body had my back arched, my toes curled, and the world turning red. Every inch of me burned, for him, for me. Didn't matter. My world was on fire, and I loved it. Without thought, surrendering to the need I felt from him, I bit him back, sinking my teeth into the flesh of his shoulder. He bucked and groaned, stomach hard against mine, shaking as his own orgasm took over. Joined in more ways than one, coming together as we came apart.

"Fuck," I whispered as my haze faded and reality came barging back in. "I can *feel* you."

Shadow grunted, licking my neck as he teased me with long strokes of his hands. "I'm still inside you, so I sure as hell hope so."

I rolled my eyes. "Not that."

He hummed. "I know." He pulled back, looking down at me, smiling. "I can feel you, too."

"The thread's wrapped around us tight," I whispered, closing my eyes as my pull to him tugged, my heart skipping with the completion of it.

"I like tight." He pushed his hips into mine, making me giggle. "Hold that thought, though. I need to take care of this."

He slid out of me, holding the condom at the base of his still-hard cock as he hurried into the bathroom. How he could not be as deflated as a cheap tire on a glass-strewn highway, I had no idea. Maybe some kind of shifter magick. Something dirty and obscene…and perfect.

I stretched and grabbed the sheet, covering myself as I snuggled into Shadow's pillows. He quickly rejoined me, waiting as I held up the covers for him to crawl under. To join me and snuggle together. Something I loved doing with him.

"What time do you leave in the morning?" he asked as he

settled himself around me. I curled into his hold, sighing at how warm and comfortable it was to be caged by this man.

"Early. The girls want to be on the road at five so we can be at Merriweather by ten at the latest. The carnival is supposed to open at four, and we need to make sure everything is set."

He kissed my temple, my cheek, nibbling my ear. "It's going to be a long day for you."

"And for you." I tilted my head back, enticing him to my neck, knowing how much he loved nuzzling me there. "Doesn't the ride start at like nine?"

"Yeah, we're supposed to be in Kalamazoo for lunch, then we'll ride the rest of the way to Chicago."

"That's a long ride," I said, rubbing my fingers across his chest.

Shadow hummed. "It's not like I haven't done it before and won't have to do it again."

His words made me pause, my heart beating fast. My words soft. "Will you be coming back with the rest of the guys after the celebration?"

Shadow went quiet, his arms squeezing me tighter, holding me to him in a way that said more than his words could. "Probably not. There's still some things to be done, and I need to help Jameson track down those loose threads we left dangling."

"How long?" I asked, my heart aching at the thought of being away from him again.

"I don't know." He pulled back, meeting my gaze with warm eyes. "But this time, I'll call every day. We'll text all the time, too. And I promise to ride as hard and fast as I can to get back to you once I get a break."

I sighed, knowing that was really the best I could ask for. He had a job built on secrets, ones he had to keep even from me. I could accept that as long as I knew he was safe. As long as I knew he'd come back to me. Though I had to admit, the idea of Shadow speeding through the night on his low-slung motorcycle to get to me was an exciting vision. One that made me wonder what it'd be like to ride on the back of his bike. Which made me think about...

"Does your ass get sore when you ride?"

Shadow paused, silent and still as if actually considering my question. "No, not really."

"Huh."

"Why, huh?"

I shrugged. "I just thought it might be a nice way to end the day."

He pulled back, looking down at me. "What might?"

"Well, we won't see each other during the day since I'm going with the girls to set up. And then I'm coming back first thing the next morning after the celebration carnival while you go off to do secret-agent-shifter stuff." I smiled, pulling him closer, letting my hands warm as I stroked up and down his back. "I thought it might be fun to spend the evening taking advantage of the rides and games at the fair."

"Well, yeah," he said, obviously confused. "We'll hang out at the fair with everyone else."

"Right." I pushed him to his back and sat up, straddling his hips, rubbing myself against where he was hard and thick still, secretly thanking my lucky stars for that ability. "And then, when the PG-rated fun is over, I was thinking I could spend some NC-17 time rubbing out the soreness from your ride."

"Oh," he whispered, staring up at me, biting his lip as I moved against him. "I'm down for that. I'll definitely be sore enough for a rubdown."

"Really?" I leaned down to capture his lips with mine as I reached for the open box of condoms. Ready for another round. Hell, ready for ten more rounds.

"Definitely." He closed his eyes and tossed his head back as I sheathed him. Such a sexy vision, giving himself to me.

Letting me take over. Letting me do what I wanted. And what I wanted was for him to be inside me.

Without pause, I lined him up and slid down, groaning at the way he stretched me, loving the way he filled me so completely. Every inch of me tingling from the bond we'd formed only moments before.

"Good," I whispered, licking my top lip and working my hips in a slow circle. "Then your ass is mine tomorrow night."

He gripped my hips, arching into me. "Every night."

"Greedy man."

He opened his eyes, staring up at me, completely open and honest. "You like it."

I leaned down again, swiveling my hips as I gave his plump bottom lip a nibble. "I love it."

TWENTY-ONE

Shadow

THE K-ZOO DENHOUSE LOOKED like a chaotic mess when we rolled onto the lot, but the energy was lighthearted and fun. Human and shifter alike walked the lot, grabbing food, taking part in a little easy drinking. We had about an hour before the various segments of riders would start the last half of the journey to Chicago. Plenty of time to have a drink before hitting the road again, especially for the shifters in the group.

"Want a beer?" Phoenix asked as he set his helmet on the seat of his bobber.

"Yeah, that'd be great."

"Cool." He whistled, drawing the attention of a youngish looking man. "Yo, Spank. Grab us a couple of bottles, all right?"

"Sure," the kid said with a shrug. "Be right back."

I glanced from one to the other. "You know him?"

"Sort of." Phoenix grinned, looking just a bit wicked. "Just…don't shake his hand."

I had no time to ask what he meant because Rebel and Beast walked up, full of smiles and good attitude.

"Good ride, guys?" Rebel asked, his eyes inspecting us.

"Yeah, of course." Phoenix smiled and crossed his arms. "How's the bagger been handling?"

"Like a dream," Rebel said, glancing at his huge ride. "She's like a mattress on wheels."

"Speaking of mattresses," Phoenix said with a smirk. "I hear Miss Scarlett hasn't been spending a whole lot of time at home the past few nights. Do I need to have a talk with you about your intentions for my almost sister-in-law?"

I sat back against my XA, crossing my booted feet at the ankles. "So she likes hanging out with me. And?"

Beast joined Phoenix, the two grinning. "And...how's that going for you?"

I raised an eyebrow as Rebel busted up laughing. "Are we really about to do this?"

Beast and Phoenix looked at each other and nodded in unison before turning back to me. "Yes. We are."

Spank ran up and handed me a beer before disappearing back into the crowd. I pointed the bottle at the two shifters trying to bust my balls.

"You two are a couple of gossips."

Before they could answer, Gates came storming up, a worried frown on his face. "Anyone seen Princess?"

"Yeah," Beast said, pointing toward the denhouse. "She said she was headed inside to use the restroom."

"Oh." Gates glanced in that direction, his frown not disappearing. "Thanks."

As Gates left us behind, the joking started again. All three guys trying their best to wheedle secrets about the fire witch out of me. Not that I was telling them a damn thing.

"C'mon, man, you're newly mated." Beast smirked, and I knew whatever was coming was going to be bad enough to never repeat to Scarlett. "I know exactly how a newly mated wolf feels. But we're all curious... How hot does that fire magic make her? What level of burnt is your dick right now? Slightly pink, or charred and crispy?"

I groaned as the guys laughed, cutting up and using me as the butt of their jokes. Not that I minded. I'd take any ribbing necessary as long as it meant my mate was in my life.

"You know," said Klutch as he joined us, his fiery red hair a standout in the crowd. "Turnabout is fair play. What about you, Phoenix... What's it like getting it on with a siren?"

Phoenix's face went slack before his cheeks ruddied. Blushing. The kid was blushing. That alone was worth all the hassle they'd given me.

"Are you fucking blushing?" Beast asked, howling with laughter.

"You just...don't...the one time." He blew out a breath, glaring at Klutch. "Don't let her sing near the water. Trust me on that one."

Our laughter boomed, the only thing that could have interrupted it being the growling of a very pissed off Gates. He stalked to us, his eyes wild, fingertips curled in a way that meant his claws were coming out. Ending the easy vibe we'd been enjoying. Each of us tensed, sensing his upset, his fear.

"She's not in there," Gates said, shaking his head. "She's near, but my mating bond to her is..."

"What? What's wrong with your bond?" Rebel asked, suddenly serious. It was easy to forget at times with how close we all were, but Rebel was the president of our group. If anything happened to one of us, technically, he was responsible. That was a heavy weight to carry, one he took seriously.

"I don't know." Gates shook his head, looking around the crowd again. "But something isn't right. I can feel it."

The first ring sounded from Rebel's pocket, the rest of our phones echoing in a chorus of alerts. Text messages, emails, voice mails. The phones of every shifter in the group came alive within two seconds of one another, sending my thoughts spiraling, my stomach dropping into a pit of dread.

"What the hell," Rebel said, reading his screen. His face fell, his eyes going wide as he looked up to the rest of us. One by one, we each read our message or listened to our voice mail.

Crash, the leader of the K-zoo den just under Rebel's level of authority, raced up, interrupting our stunned silence. "Shit, Rebel. The president's home is under attack."

"Full-blown SOS at Merriweather Fields," Klutch whispered, the wonder in his voice something we all had to be feeling. "I don't think that's ever happened before."

I swallowed hard, my every thought focused in over a hundred miles west of where I stood. It took huge, brass balls to attack the home base of the NALB president. The very building where Scarlett and her sisters were supposed to be finalizing carnival plans for the end of the ride.

"Where are the girls?" Phoenix asked. I dragged my attention to his face, the two of us probably looking like carbon copies of each other. Pale, scared, the reality of the situation hitting us hard.

"They're at Merriweather," Rebel whispered. "They were staying there for lunch with Blaze's mate, Moira, before heading over to the fairgrounds."

"Motherfucker," I hissed, dialing Scarlett's number.

Suddenly Gates roared, a sound there would be no way to truly explain to the humans who turned to figure out what had made it. A sound that made the hairs on the back of my neck stand up.

"She's gone." He stalked toward his bike. "The bond is fading, but I can sense her fear. Someone's taken her."

"Toward Chicago?" Rebel asked.

"West," Gates said, his eyes unfocused as he stared toward the highway. "So far, I feel her going west."

Rebel grabbed Crash by the arm. "I need the keys to a war wagon. Now."

Crash nodded once and yelled, "Spank."

The boy appeared, looking terrified.

"Get me the keys to the Suburbans. And move your ass." Crash turned back to Rebel as the boy ran off. "What else?"

"Grab every hanger-on you can find and have them keep this party going. When it's time to leave, they need to lead the ride to the fairgrounds. Keep it slow. I don't want a single human to figure out there's a problem."

"On it."

"We're heading to the Fields now," Rebel said, gripping the keys to his bagger. "Get every Feral Breed member out there. Our president is in trouble, along with our mates. You tell those fuckers they'd better ride hard and fast; we're two and a half hours away and they need us."

Spank appeared, holding two sets of keys in his hands. "Gray and black."

"Thanks," Rebel said. He grabbed the set for the gray and tossed it to Gates, handing the black ones to Crash. "Gates, Klutch, and Beast will head after Kaija. If it takes you to the Fields, so be it. If not, do what you have to do to get her back. Call in for whatever help you need."

"No," Beast said, taking a step back. "I'm sorry, brother, but I can't. Calla and Aliyana are at the Fields. I won't be able to think clearly knowing they're in danger."

Gates stared at his brother, growling, crazed-looking, before he sighed and nodded. "Understood. Go get my niece."

Beast hugged him hard, whispering a few quiet words in Spanish before racing for his chopper, not bothering to toss on his helmet.

"Numbers," Rebel yelled, catching the attention of another denmate. "You go with Gates and Klutch."

The three men disappeared, following Spank to the side lot where the war wagons—two giant SUVs with tinted windows, stocked to the roof with weapons and medical supplies—sat parked.

Rebel gave one last look over the lot before shaking his head. "The timing makes me think they planned this, knowing the Breed would be busy with the rides to Merriweather and the celebration for Blaze's birthday."

I swung a leg over my bike, dialing Scarlett again, ready to roll but holding out hope for an answer. "Scarlett hasn't texted for a few hours. Have you heard from Charlotte?"

Rebel glanced at his phone. "Yeah, she texted me like forty minutes ago talking about some big freak-out Amber had."

A chill crept down my spine, a sense of foreboding worthy of the air witch herself. "What kind of freak-out?"

Rebel shrugged. "Something about the carousel Dante requested for the carnival."

"Motherfucker," I hissed, starting my bike. "Amber said to stay off the carousel during one of her visions, something about smoke."

"Shit," Rebel said, running a hand roughly over his head. "We need to go. Head out, I'll catch up."

I nodded, images of flame-tipped dark hair sprawled across my chest making my heart hurt and my gut clench in fear. Thank God I could feel her so I knew she was at least alive. I just needed to get to her. To keep her safe.

"The Cleaners will be there," I said, ready to make a call for the girls.

Rebel shook his head, looking angry and frustrated. "I know where your head is, but that's a no. Their job isn't to save our mates or our brothers. They're all about Blaze. Our mates are unprotected."

My growl came up hard and fast, more of a tiger's roar than a wolf growl as my frustration crested. Over two hours...too far to do much more than hope she could handle herself enough to hold out for me. Rebel's eyes went wide, but he didn't comment as my arms darkened with stripes, my tiger claws punching through my fingertips.

I pressed redial for Scarlett's number one more time as I hefted the bike to a full stand. Phoenix and Rebel raced for their own rides, heavy bootsteps breaking through the jovial sounds of the crowd of people who had no idea our worlds were collapsing. I cursed as Scarlett's phone went directly to voice mail, ready to throw the fucking phone in the woods. "She's not picking up."

Rebel shook his head, his own phone in his hand as he mounted the blue and white bike he'd had designed when he met his mate. "Neither is Charlotte."

"Zuri either." Phoenix started his engine, ready to roll. "Or Calla."

My stomach sank, knowing how much was on the line. "They're all there. Even Amber, Jameson, and the Appalachian shifters. Omega Kalie was still in the infirmary last time I talked to Jameson."

Rebel smashed his fist into his thigh and hissed, "Goddammit. Ride...now!"

I nodded and kicked off, pulling out onto the highway heading west, clinging tightly to the hope that my girl could defend herself if need be. She had her sisters, and they had their magick. But Calla and Charlotte were human; they had no special skills to fight off a wolf shifter ready to take them out. Plus there was a baby added into the mix—technically a shifter, but too young to be more than an easy target for an enemy. Thankfully, our girls were close, tight. They'd keep each other safe for as long as they could. But with one pregnant and another with a small baby to guard, their options would be limited. We needed to bust ass to back them up.

JUST UNDER TWO HOURS later, we screamed off the tollway and onto the road that would take us to Merriweather Fields. This was a relatively residential area, with houses and small businesses lining the streets. On a normal day, we'd cruise through at a calm thirty-five so as not to ruffle the locals' feathers.

This was not a normal day.

I took the exit ramp at ninety-five, revving hard for the straightaway after the loop. Phoenix rode right on my tail, Rebel leading the way. They had to be just as worried as I was. Even though I could feel Scarlett, knew she was alive and the general area of where she was, the worry over how much trouble she was in consumed me. I needed to get to her, to drive faster, to figure out a way to teleport. I needed to be by her side.

We were rolling toward the river we'd need to cross to reach the road that would take us into the downtown area of the little city Merriweather technically occupied when a sharp tug inside my chest made me look south. Toward the woods. Toward the river as it curved through the trees.

Toward what looked like a water spout wrapped in flames swirling between the leafy canopies.

I stared for about two seconds, Scarlett's own words from our date coming back to me.

"If you ever see what looks like a water tornado on fire, you can trust it's Zuri and me screwing around."

Somehow, I doubted they were screwing around, but that was definitely my mate and her sisters.

Without conscious thought on the matter, I leaped for the trees. My bike fell and skidded down the road, sparks flying and metal screeching as the engine continued to rev. I didn't care. All thoughts were gone, all focus handed over to pure animal instinct.

I shifted in midair from human to beast, rolling through the change with practiced ease. Landing on the grass at the side of the road, I raced ahead without pause, stripes out and a roar booming from my mouth.

My tiger had taken control.

I felt more than saw Phoenix and Rebel behind me, their canine energy slightly at odds with the feline power flowing through me. But it didn't matter, they didn't matter. All I could see, all I cared about, was moving faster. Getting to the base of that water spout. Getting to my mate.

As I ran past the final curve before the river, the site of the carnival came into view. An old church camp with shabby white buildings and a pool at the front sat at the bottom of a small hill. The rides were scattered about the property—Ferris wheel, Zipper, mini-roller coaster, lots of spinny things for little kids to play on, and a huge, sparkling carousel. Not yet surrounded by smoke. Had I been human, I would have sighed in relief.

Until I broke through the final line of trees and got a clear view of the midway.

There, just along the edge of the river, a line of at least ten wolves stalked toward the base of the swirling spout. Inside, past the whirling air and the dirt and the fire, five women stood in a circle. Hands joined, hair flying in the wind.

One covered in flames.

I leaped over the tall fence surrounding the camp and raced down the hill. My mate—my beautiful, strong, powerful mate—had set herself on fire to save her sisters and the other two women with them. I recognized one as Charlotte. My heart sank as the fifth turned and glanced my way. Lanie…sister-in-law to Kaija, the human mate of one of her brothers. Three witches and two humans standing against a dozen shifters. How the girls lasted to this point, I had no idea, but I'd make sure they stayed safe. All of them.

I leaped through the rotating wind around them, coming to stand beside Scarlett as soon as I landed. I growled and looked up at her through my animal eyes, not feeling pain through our bond but peace. Calmness. Magick.

"It's about time you got here," she said, her voice strong and filled with sarcasm even as her hair glowed and the fire flew from her fingers. "I was beginning to think we'd have to handle all these guys alone."

I growled and rubbed my head against her thigh, singeing my whiskers. She bumped me with her hip, her hands still up and out, flames and heat radiating off her. But that was all the time I had. Two wolves rushed the funnel, making everyone inside take a step back. Zuri swung her arm in a circle, tossing what looked like a wave of water their way and knocking them backward into the mud.

"We can't hold them back much longer," Zuri said. Phoenix growled in wolf form at her side, staring at the line of wolves facing us. Head down, hackles up, he challenged every wolf out there to try him. To attempt it. To dare to come at him. Phoenix was a big wolf, bigger than almost all I'd ever seen, and right then, he looked positively unstoppable.

"What do we do?" Charlotte asked. Rebel circled her like a caged animal, ready to fight. Ready to defend. Which was a good thing. Because a full breach of the Fields and the number of wolves facing us down could only mean one thing.

War had come, and our mates were smack dab in the middle of it.

"We fight," Scarlett said, looking into my eyes with a fierceness that rivaled my own. "We fight until we win."

A shifter who thought he'd lost it all.

A woman far too familiar with death.

A fate worth dying for.

CLAIMING HIS DESIRE

FERAL BREED MOTORCYCLE CLUB
BOOK SIX

ACKNOWLEDGMENTS

As always, I have to say thank you to the readers of the Feral Breed. You keep me energized and on task. You also make me giggle and blush...especially you wild ones from the Feral Breed Reader Group.

To Lisa, who happens to be the greatest editor a gal could ask for and one hell of a friend.

To Caren, Esher, and Anna, who continually challenge me and my writing. They're my safety nets.

To Brighton, for holding my figurative hand through my first conference.

And to my husband, for sending me the best text messages and reminding me why I work so hard.

Edited by Silently Correcting Your Grammar, LLC
Cover Art by Cormar Covers

ABOUT THE AUTHOR

A storyteller from the time she could talk, Ellis grew up among family legends of hauntings, psychics, and love spanning decades. Those stories didn't always have the happiest of endings, so they inspired her to write about real life, real love, and the difficulties therein. From farmers to werewolves, store clerks to witches—if there's love to be found, she'll write about it. Ellis lives in the Chicago area with her husband, daughters, and a giant dog who hogs the bed.

Find Ellis online at:
Website: www.ellisleigh.com
Twitter: https://twitter.com/ellis_writes
Facebook: https://www.facebook.com/ellisleighwrites

CPSIA information can be obtained at www.ICGtesting.com
Printed in the USA
BVOW08s1236180715

408923BV00001B/44/P